EC
EDEN
COLLEGE

ELLA AT EDEN

For all the gymnasts out there,
especially our friends at Aussie Gems.

Scholastic Australia
An imprint of Scholastic Australia Pty Limited
PO Box 579 Gosford NSW 2250
ABN 11 000 614 577
www.scholastic.com.au

Part of the Scholastic Group
Sydney • Auckland • New York • Toronto • London • Mexico City • New Delhi • Hong Kong • Buenos Aires • Puerto Rico

Published by Scholastic Australia in 2023.

Cover and internal illustrations by Danielle McDonald.

NATIONAL LIBRARY OF AUSTRALIA
A catalogue record for this book is available from the National Library of Australia

ISBN: 978-1-76120-732-7

Typeset in Carniola

Printed in China by Hang Tai Printing Company Limited.

MIX
Paper | Supporting responsible forestry
FSC® C023121
FSC www.fsc.org
This product is made of material from well-managed FSC®-certified forests, recycled material and other controlled sources.

26 27 28 / 2

EDEN COLLEGE

ELLA AT EDEN

Perfect Score

LAURA SIEVEKING

A Scholastic Australia book

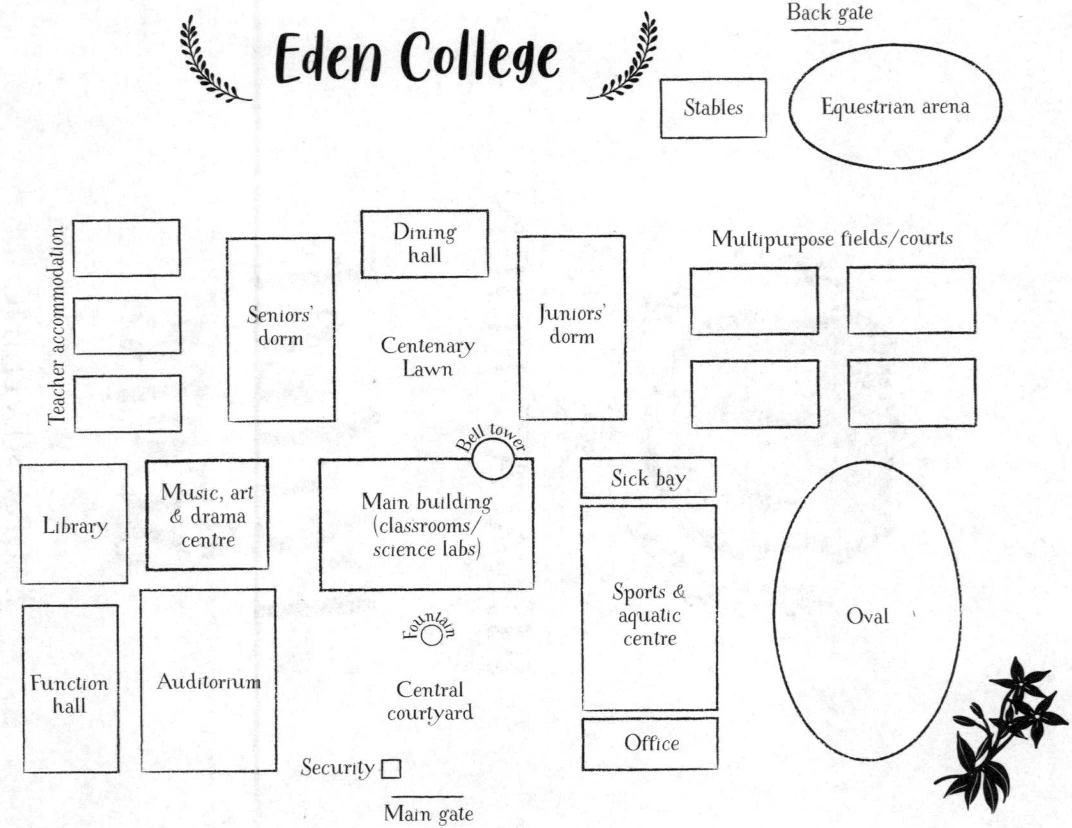
Eden College
Back gate
Stables
Equestrian arena
Teacher accommodation
Seniors' dorm
Dining hall
Centenary Lawn
Juniors' dorm
Multipurpose fields/courts
Bell tower
Library
Music, art & drama centre
Main building (classrooms/ science labs)
Sick bay
Sports & aquatic centre
Oval
Fountain
Function hall
Auditorium
Central courtyard
Office
Security
Main gate

Juniors' Dorm

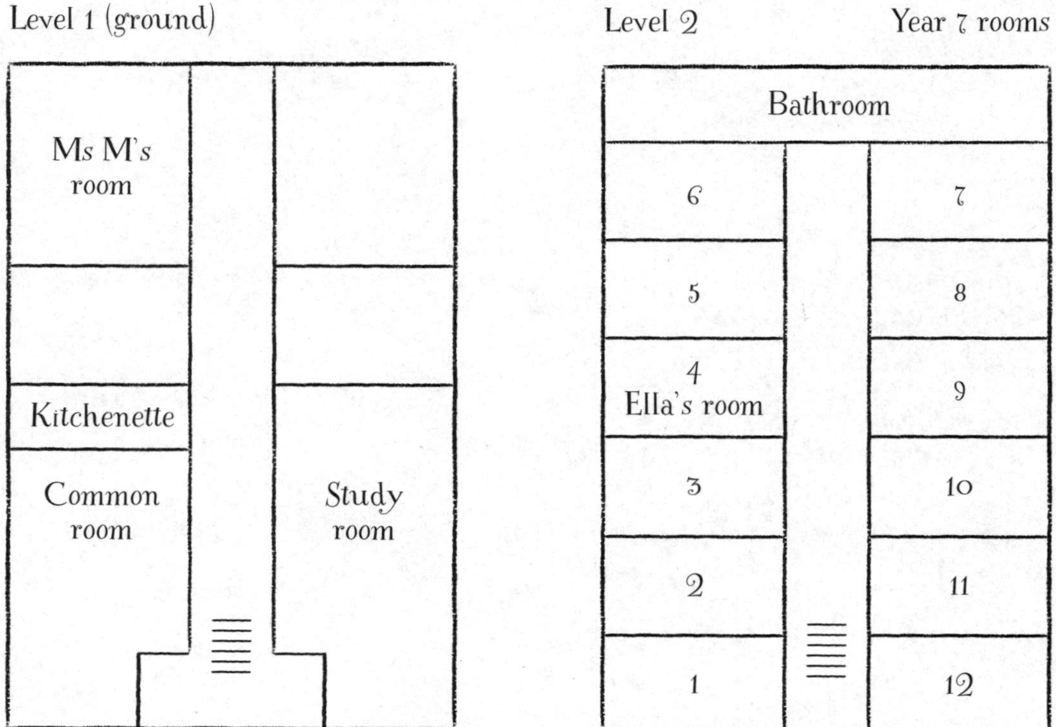

Chapter 1

'Ella, you need to push off the mat harder. Really push through your shoulders or you won't get the height needed for your back somersault,' Coach Marie said. 'Try it again.'

I nodded and walked back up the mats. I love tumbling. It's one of my favourite things to do in gymnastics. I thought about the Interschool Gymnastics Championships, which was only a month away. For Level 6, the floor tumbling row is a roundoff, back handspring and back somersault. My back handspring was ready but I wasn't quite getting the height on my back somersault, which meant I always landed in a crouch with my hands on the mat instead of sticking my landing and standing tall.

I turned back down the mat to face Coach Marie, who was standing at the end of the tumbling run, ready to jump in if we needed help. I took a deep breath and focused my attention on what I needed to do. I pounced into action and ran down the mat, reaching my hands out in front of me for my roundoff. I pushed hard off the mat through my shoulders like Coach Marie instructed, and did a long and clean back handspring. I then pulled my body up high and tucked it into a ball for a back somersault. I rotated through the air and landed in a slight crouch, but managed to keep upright without resting my hands on the mat for balance.

'Much better!' Coach Marie beamed.

She gave me a high-five and I smiled back at her.

I returned to the start of the mats and my gym friends gave a cheer. It was the first time I'd landed a back sommie without putting my hands down.

'Go Ella!' Mia said, giving me a fist-bump as

I re-joined the line.

Mia was in Year 8 and had become a good friend of mine in the gym. We trained three afternoons a week together, and sometimes on the weekend if we had a competition coming up. We both compete at Level 6, so we have become really close over my time at Eden College. Mia's green eyes sparkled as she turned to focus on her own tumbling row. She gently tucked a stray piece of hair into her tight bun.

'Come on, Mia,' Coach Marie said, clapping her hands together.

Mia thundered down the mats and launched herself into a strong roundoff, followed by a long back handspring. She pushed off the mats and soared through the air, tucking her legs up into a somersault. As she came out, she twisted her body and opened out facing the other way.

'Hey, the routine is just a back sommie, not a back sommie with a twist!' Coach Marie said, pretending to be annoyed.

Mia flashed a cheeky smile at Coach Marie and

jogged back up the mats.

'Show-off,' I teased, giving her a playful push.

'How do you manage to make it look so *easy*?' Charlotte said.

Charlotte was in Year 9 but also competing at Level 6 with me and Mia, so we hung out a lot at training. She scrunched up her nose in jovial frustration at Mia's ability to do everything in gym with ease.

Mia shrugged. 'I find floor easy. But I'm not good at *everything*,' she laughed.

'Oh, name one apparatus you are not good at!' Jasmine challenged her with raised eyebrows.

Jasmine was in Year 8 with Mia and they were really close. They hung out at school and gym, so they definitely saw a lot of each other.

'Vault,' Mia said, frowning. 'Vault is always out to get me!'

We all nodded and smiled in agreement, because Mia was actually right. She was OK at vault, but it definitely wasn't her strongest apparatus. And she often struggled to land it. But that was still only one tiny thing—everything else she did at the gym was practically perfect.

'Less chat, more work!' Coach Marie yelled from the other end of the mats.

It was now Charlotte's turn. She was working on a forward tumbling row, which was a front handspring, quickly followed by a front somersault. She ran down the mat and launched into a strong handspring, but her sommie was too low and she landed on her bottom with a thump. She grimaced as Coach Marie helped her up.

'Quick, try again,' Coach Marie said, pointing towards the start of the mats. 'Don't want to end on a fall,' she winked.

Charlotte jogged back and tried again, and achieved a front handspring with enough height that she landed her sommie. Coach Marie patted her on the back.

'OK, girls,' Coach Marie said, walking down the mats towards us. 'Good job today. Make sure you do a warm down, then head back to the dorms.'

We moved to the centre of the floor mats and sat down. The girls from the other levels joined us and began their own warm downs. I shifted into a seated straddle and stretched my arms out towards my left foot, holding the stretch so I could feel it up the back of the leg. Then I stretched the other side.

After I'd done both sides, I kept my legs out wide but pressed my body against the floor so that I was lying flat. This was called the 'pancake' stretch because the aim was to get as flat as a pancake!

I turned my head sideways so I could see my friends. The other girls stretched at their own pace while we chatted.

'How many weeks until Interschools?' Jasmine asked.

'About four,' I said.

'We have so much work to do!' Charlotte moaned. 'I still have to stick my back walkover on the beam, fix my floor tumbling and stick my flyaway on bars.'

To *stick* something in gymnastics means to complete a landing without stepping or moving your feet for balance. It takes a lot of practice and great technique!

'You'll get there,' Mia said kindly. 'We've all got something to work on. I don't think I've stuck a landing on my vault this week!'

It was true. In Women's Artistic Gymnastics, which is our discipline of the sport, there are the uneven bars, floor, vault and beam, and everyone has their favoured apparatus. But everyone also has at least one nemesis. A *nemesis* is an archenemy that is always out to get you. For me, it was the back walkover on the balance beam. I was terrified of bending backwards onto my hands on such a tiny plank of wood!

I slipped into side splits, wincing slightly at the deep stretch.

Mia, of course, sat in her splits as if it was the most comfortable position in the world.

'Mia, into oversplit, please,' Coach Marie yelled from the other side of the gym.

Mia rolled her eyes and stood up to get her blocks. Oversplits is what a gymnast does if the splits is too easy for them. Instead of having their legs on the floor, the front leg rests on top of a block to make it harder. Mia was so flexible that she could put her front leg up on three stacked blocks and still get her splits down to the ground. I wouldn't attempt an oversplit because I wasn't flexible enough, and you can really hurt yourself if you try it before you are ready.

We finished up our stretching and helped Coach Marie tidy up the gym. Then we grabbed our training bags and slung them over our shoulders so we could walk back to the dorms.

'Walk with us, Ella?' Jasmine asked, as she headed for the door.

Because we were all in years 7 to 9, we lived in the same dormitory house.

'See you later, Mia!' Charlotte called out.

Mia waved goodbye. She wasn't coming back to the dorm with us, as she didn't live there like we did—she lived in a house on the Eden campus with her mum.

'Let's go, Mia,' Coach Marie said, hurrying her along.

'Coming, Mum,' Mia replied, rolling her eyes lightly.

As they walked away, I could hear Coach Marie telling her daughter where she needed to fix up her routines a bit more. Mia nodded while she listened, but she wasn't smiling.

I tilted my head to the side, deep in thought.

'Ella? You coming?' Charlotte called.

I nodded my head and followed Jasmine and Charlotte back to the dorms.

Chapter 2

The spring sun sunk deep into my skin, warming me all over. It was nice to be back in our summer dresses after the cold winter, and to breathe in the smell of gardenia as it filled the air. The best part about the warmer months was that we could eat our lunch and afternoon tea outside. I didn't like being cooped up inside the dining hall all through winter.

As I sat in the sun, I pulled off my black school shoes and slipped off my socks to wriggle my toes in the grass. It was the end of the day and the usual school time restrictions around uniform didn't apply. My friends,

Grace, Zoe, Violet and Ariel, had also pulled off their shoes and socks and were enjoying the spring warmth.

'Hats, girls,' a curt voice called from behind us.

Ms Montgomery, the school vice-headmistress was strolling past us on her way back to the dorms.

'Yes, Ms Montgomery,' we chorused. While the rules were more relaxed after school hours, hats were still required outside, so we each put our broad brimmed hats back on our heads.

The Panama hat had to be worn when we were out on excursions or sitting outside in the sun. I knew it was to stop us getting burnt, but the stiff tightly woven hat wasn't the most comfortable thing I'd ever worn.

When Ms Montgomery was out of sight, Grace pulled hers off and began to throw it into the air, catching it again on its way down.

I pulled the paper lining off the blueberry muffin I had picked up from the dining hall for afternoon tea. Ariel peeled a banana and Violet bit into her specially-made slice which was diabetic-friendly.

'I can't believe we are over halfway through Year 7,'

Zoe said wistfully as she gazed up at the clear blue sky. 'We've almost been at Eden for an entire year.'

I thought about that. On one level, it felt like the year so far had zoomed by like a runaway train. But on another level, it felt like I'd lived at the college for half my life. It felt like there had never been a time that I hadn't known Grace, Violet and Ariel, even though I'd only met them all at the beginning of the year. We'd become as close as sisters, coming together with our own personalities and struggles, just like anybody else at the school. Zoe has been my BFF since we were four years old. She was steadfast and dependable. Violet was kind and gentle and the perfect person to talk to if you had something on your mind. Ariel was newer to the college, but I'd gotten to know her as a funny and quirky friend, and not as the famous child-movie actress she was. She always knew what to say to make you laugh when you were down. And then there was Grace. Grace with all her crazy ideas and daring personality. It was like she wasn't afraid of anything and never seemed to get beaten down by the worries of the world. Sometimes

I wished I was a little more like Grace. I had a tendency to overthink things which could make me a bit of a worry-wart, as my Nanna Kate would say.

'There's still so much left to do though,' Violet said, finishing her slice. 'I've got so many end-of-year concerts coming up next term for singing.'

'I have one more Maths Olympiad,' Zoe added.

'And I've got a drama piece for the spring concert,' Ariel said.

'Oh, yeah, and I'm meant to help paint the set for that!' Grace added, slapping her forehead. 'I forgot all about that one!' She shook her head and frowned. I cocked my head to the side, looking at my friend. She usually didn't let it bother her when she forgot something, but now she seemed really annoyed at herself. She shook her head again, as if trying to shake the frustration away.

'I'm pretty nervous about the Interschool Gymnastics Competition coming up in a month,' I said, gently chewing my lower lip.

'Why so nervous? You're great at gym,' Ariel said,

playing with a blade of grass between her fingers.

'I have to fix up a few things in my routines.' I said. 'Especially my back walkover on the beam.' The very thought of it made my leg jitter up and down.

'What's that?' Violet asked.

'It's a back-bend followed by a kick over,' I said, standing up. I stretched my arms tall to the sky and then bent backwards, leading with my shoulders. My hands touched the grass and I kicked my legs over the top until I was standing tall again.

'That looked pretty easy for you,' Grace said. 'What's the problem?'

'You try that on a beam, which is only 10cm wide,' I said. 'It's terrifying!'

Zoe shuddered. 'And *that's* why I don't do gym,' she laughed.

'Yet you'll ride a horse at break-neck speed?' I challenged.

Zoe laughed. 'Truth!'

I guess we all had our own talents and fears.

Grace looked up and her usual mischievous glint

returned to her eyes. She tossed her Panama hat across to Zoe, yelling, 'Catch!'

Zoe caught it and flung it back.

'Don't let Monty see you throwing your hat around,' Violet warned.

'Ariel, go long!' Grace yelled, standing up and gesturing for Ariel to run across the grass.

Ariel stood up and bolted across the lawn as Grace threw the hat roughly. It sailed through the air like a UFO and Ariel caught it, giggling.

'These things may be the most uncomfortable hats on earth, but they make awesome flying saucers!' Grace said, catching her hat as Ariel threw it back.

At that moment, Saskia and her friends, Portia and Mercedes, came into view. Saskia had her long blonde hair pulled up into a bun and she had a towel draped over her shoulder. She'd either been at swimming squad or the girls had gone for an after-school leisure swim, which was always allowed in the warmer months.

'Hey, Sass, catch!' Grace yelled, flinging her hat as hard as she could in Saskia's direction.

'Wait, what?!' Saskia yelled, not expecting a Panama hat to come hurtling through the air towards her head. On instinct, she ducked.

An unexpected breeze then whipped Grace's hat up into the air and it sailed up into a tree behind Saskia, where it lodged itself into one of the top branches.

'Haha!' Saskia laughed, pointing to the hat.

I looked up at Grace and shook my head. 'Now what?'

'I'll have to get it!' Grace sang, hitching her dress up and tucking it into the legs of the bike pants she wore underneath.

'I can't look,' Violet said, wincing.

We all watched as Grace scaled the tree. She pulled herself up the first branch and reached for the second. She climbed up and up until she was near the top of the tree. When she reached the final branch, she stood on her tiptoes and jumped to reach it. She then hauled herself up to where her hat was.

'Got it!' she yelled, flinging her hat down to the grass below.

Grace looked from side to side. She frowned.

'Um, how do I get down?' she asked.

Saskia cackled and walked away, with Portia and Mercedes trailing behind her.

'Hang down to the below branch,' Ariel called.

'But my feet don't reach—I jumped from that one. I don't want to drop onto it—I might fall!' Grace called.

'Don't you think you should have thought about that before you decided to climb the tree?' Violet yelled.

'Grace! What are you doing up there?' an angry voice called from behind us.

Ms Montgomery.

'Oh, um, just taking in the view,' Grace said, looking out over the trees.

'Get down at once!' Ms Montgomery yelled.

'Yeah, about that,' Grace said airily. 'Seems like I'm a bit . . . stuck.'

Ms Montgomery's face reddened in anger. She sighed and marched off to get the caretaker who would have a ladder. In the meantime, we were instructed to remain at the base of the tree and to not let Grace attempt to get down by herself.

'Grace, you are in so much trouble when Monty gets you down,' Zoe said.

Grace shrugged. 'I'll get out of it. I always do. It's my *charm.*'

Grace was right. She *did* have a way of getting out of trouble. Even though she was often in detention, the teachers knew she didn't mean any harm and she never got into any real trouble. But at that moment, as the caretaker carried the ladder over to the tree and Ms Montgomery followed with what looked like steam coming out of her ears, I thought maybe Grace had just used up her ninth life.

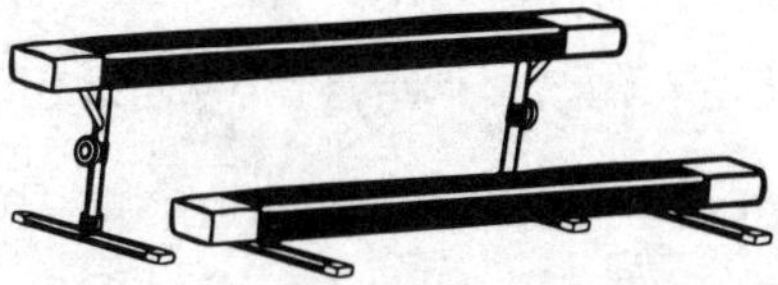

Chapter 3

From: Ella

Sent: Thursday, 6:08 AM

To: Olivia

Subject: Good morning!

Hi Olivia,

It's so early! I should still be asleep, but with only 4 weeks until Interschools we are now doing gymnastics training in the morning as well as in the afternoon. I feel tired already! I'm just waiting for Charlotte and Jasmine to come down, so I thought I'd send you a quick email.

How's it going? How was school camp?? Did anyone vomit on the bus? That's always the worst bit.

I'm trying to work on my back walkover on the beam but it's absolutely petrifying. That means scary to the power of a million, in case you didn't know. I'm so scared my hands will fall off the beam and I'll do an epic face plant. But I want to get it right because the Interschools comp is a team competition, so my score will be added to the other Level 6 scores, and if I stuff it up I'll have let my team down. And I don't want to do that, no way!

The comp is at a big gymnastics centre on the coast. And the best part is that we get to go to the beach during our time off! It's held on a Saturday and we all compete across the four apparatus. Our team's individual scores are added together for a school total, and then the best school is crowned the champion. There are different segments for Artistic and Rhythmic gymnastics (rhythmic is the one with the ribbons and balls and all that stuff) and there is a boys' comp running at the same time.

Coach Marie said she has a surprise for us at training this

morning—whatever that means! I hope it involves lollies, but I bet it doesn't.

Talk to you later!

Ella xx

PS I'll call you this afternoon. I was meant to be hanging out with Grace but now she's got detention for throwing her hat into a tree. Long story.

'I want you all focusing on your weakest apparatus this morning,' Coach Marie said after we'd all done our warm up. 'That means being responsible and getting your practice done, even when I'm not looking.'

Mia, Jasmine, Charlotte and I exchanged cheeky glances.

'Charlotte and Ella, you both need to practice your back walkovers on beam. Jasmine, you're on the bars to do fifty kips.'

'Fifty kips?!'

'Yes, fifty. And Mia, you're coming with me to vault,'

Coach Marie said flatly.

'Aaw, Mum, I don't want to do vault *again* today!' Mia protested.

'It's Coach when we're in the gym, remember?' Coach Marie said, frowning at her daughter.

Mia rolled her eyes and followed her mum over to the vault.

'We'll start with sprints,' I heard Coach Marie say as they moved to the other side of the gym.

Jasmine peeled off to the bars to start her kips, which was a special kind of swing performed on the bar.

Charlotte and I walked over to the beams.

'Poor Mia,' Charlotte said, gazing over at the vault.

'Why?' I asked.

'Imagine having your mum as a coach,' Charlotte replied.

'It'd be kind of convenient,' I said. 'She'd be able to tell you exactly what you were doing wrong.'

'Exactly my point,' Charlotte said. 'How annoying would that be?!'

I followed her gaze to the vault. Coach Marie was

doing resistance runs with Mia. She had a big band around Mia's waist and was pulling her back while Mia tried to run forwards. It made running super-duper hard, but it was awesome for building up leg muscles and speed on the run-up.

I did a couple of back walkovers on the mats next to the beam. It was easy when there was no height involved.

'Can you spot me for the first few?' Charlotte asked, standing on the lowest beam.

I nodded.

I went to the lowest beam which was only about 20cm above the floor. I could stand next to it and still be at a good height to spot Charlotte. Spotting is just a fancy gym word for helping someone complete a skill safely.

Charlotte stood tall with her hands up in the air and her arms stretched tight. She lifted one leg straight out in front of her and I put my left hand gently underneath. I then placed my other hand on her back for support. We'd been shown many times how to spot safely in a class.

Arching back, Charlotte led with her shoulders. She placed her hands down behind her then kicked her legs over so she was standing again.

'Nice!' I said, encouraging her.

Charlotte did two more before trying by herself.

She hesitated on her first attempt alone, but her confidence quickly grew and soon she was doing lots of back walkovers on the narrow beam by herself.

'Go, Charlie!' I cheered.

'Your turn,' she said, smiling cheekily.

'OK, but only on the low beam. And you spot me this time,' I said, waving her over.

I stood tall with my arms pointed towards the ceiling. Then I lifted my left leg and gently arched backwards until I felt my hands grasp the beam. Then with Charlotte's help, I kicked over.

'Good job, Ella!' she said. 'Again!'

I stood tall again and Charlotte helped me with another walkover.

'Now by yourself!' she encouraged.

It's just the low beam, I repeated to myself, *it's just the low beam*. I lifted my leg and arched backwards. But halfway through the skill I lost all my confidence. I tried to pull out of the walkover but it was too late. My body twisted and my hands missed the beam. I crumpled into a pile on the ground.

'Are you OK?' Charlotte asked, helping me up.

'Yeah,' I said. 'But imagine if that had been the high beam! I would have fallen on my head from way up there!' I pointed to the high beam.

'But you've done so many good ones on the low beam,' Charlotte said, trying to encourage me.

'No way,' I said, shaking my head. 'I'm not getting up there and doing that crazy skill. I'm out. No way. Never ever. Unsubscribe.'

Charlotte couldn't help but giggle at my dramatic response.

'Push through your shoulders!' Coach Marie yelled from the other side of the gym.

'I am!' Mia yelled back.

'Don't talk to me like that!' Coach Marie yelled. 'If you were pushing, you'd make it over the vaulting table.'

Mia shook her head angrily and took another run-up. She pumped her arms and legs and gained speed as she approached the beat board. She launched herself forward and hit the board hard with her feet. She flipped upside-down and landed onto the vaulting table in a momentary handstand. Once on the table, the idea was to push hard through your shoulders out of the handstand position and back onto your feet on the other side. But Mia's handspring sagged and she flopped over the vault like a sack of sand. She landed with a thump on her bottom.

'Ugh! I'm going to the beam!' she yelled, standing up and stomping off.

Coach Marie shook her head.

Charlotte and I exchanged worried glances as Mia came over.

'Mia, are you OK?' I asked.

She ignored me. I knew she wasn't trying to be mean. She was frustrated.

Mia jumped up onto the high beam and did a perfect back walkover all by herself. She landed it beautifully and presented with her arms.

'Wow,' I said quietly. 'You're amazing on the beam

when you're mad.'

Mia looked down at me and her frown melted into a smile. 'Well, if only my vault improved with my temper. I'd be the best vault gymnast out there.'

'Don't worry, Mia,' I said reassuringly. 'I just did an epic stack on my back walkover on the low beam. We all have our struggles.'

'Yeah, well, your mum isn't standing here in the gym watching you, expecting you to be the next Simone Biles,' Mia grimaced.

'Mia, that's not true. You know—' Charlotte began, but Mia cut her off.

'Look, I just want to do my routines,' she said, a new frown forming on her brow.

Charlotte and I awkwardly walked back over to the low beam to practice our cartwheels. I looked up at Mia's angry face as she went through a perfect beam routine. Turning, I then saw Coach Marie looking at her daughter from the other side of the room with a sad smile. But when Coach Marie caught my eye, she quickly looked away.

‘Alright, Level 6 girls, come over here,’ Coach Marie called as we finished our warm down.

The girls from other levels continued to warm down with their coaches, while the Level 6 team wandered over to Coach Marie. Coach Marie was the highest level coach in the club, so she usually looked after the upper level gymnasts, which included us. We’d be the highest level participating in the Interschools competition, so she was dedicating most of her training time on the four of us.

‘I have a little surprise for you all,’ she said with a cheeky grin.

‘What is it?’ Jasmine said, bouncing lightly on her toes.

‘As you know, the Interschools competition will be held at the sports centre on the Southern Beaches. To help you get familiar with the venue, we’ll be doing our Saturday training sessions there for the next few weeks!’

‘Oh, cool!’ Charlotte cheered. ‘They have a huge

foam pit. I can't wait to try tumbling into it!'

Our gym was a small part of the school gym, so it wasn't as big as some of the other gymnastic clubs around. And we didn't have a foam pit.

'Their sprung floor is more bouncy than ours,' Jasmine added. 'I remember it from the comp last year.'

'And,' Coach Marie added, 'I've organised for us to do a bit of training with a friend who coaches at the sports centre. He's one of the best and is an expert in strength building. I think it's exactly what you girls need to take things to the next level.'

'Will we train with his gymnasts?' Jasmine asked.

Coach Marie nodded. 'Yep. A bit of friendly competition might inspire you girls to step up!' she laughed.

'We'll smash those Southern Beaches girls easily!' I said, laughing.

'Girls?' Coach Marie repeated with a mischievous smile. 'I didn't say anything about girls.'

'What?!' we all cried in unison.

'Southern Beaches is the home to the best MAG

program in the country,' Coach Marie explained.

'What's MAG?' I asked.

Mia threw her head back in mock disgust. 'It's Men's Artistic Gymnastics!' she moaned. 'We're training with *boys*!'

Chapter 4

'I can't believe Coach Marie is making us train with boys,' I moaned. 'I mean, their gymnastics is hardly anything like our gymnastics. What's the point?'

'It won't be that bad, Ella,' Grace said, jokingly rolling her eyes.

'Yeah, well, I have a little brother and I know exactly how annoying boys can be. Not to mention the annoying boys at my old school who always pretended to be zombies,' I added.

Zoe laughed, remembering back to our primary school days. 'Braaaaaaiiins!' she groaned, her arms stretched out to imitate the boys.

I playfully threw my paper napkin at her and she threw it back.

I took a bite of the sushi roll I had picked up from the dining hall at the beginning of lunch. It was one of my favourite things on the lunch menu, and now we were back into a warmer term, it was going to be on there a lot more.

'Sounds like my brother, Alec,' Grace laughed. 'He's obsessed with this zombie space game. Every time I call him he just goes on and on about it.'

'Maybe it'll be fun training with boys,' Violet said. 'We don't see much of them here, that's for sure. Before Eden College, I was at another all-girls' school, and I have three sisters. Boys are like a foreign species to me. Even my dog is a girl!'

'Don't forget to take your rubbish with you, girls,' a voice called from behind us. It was Ms Montgomery, who always seemed to appear out of nowhere.

'Yes, Ms Montgomery,' we chorused, gathering up the stray pieces that were floating on the grass around us.

'And Grace, have you remembered the meeting in—' Ms Montgomery began.

'Yes, yes all good,' Grace interrupted abruptly.

Ms Montgomery nodded and kept walking.

'What meeting have you got with Monty?' Ariel asked Grace.

'Oh, nothing. It's just—just about . . . the other day when my hat got stuck in the tree,' Grace said dismissively.

'But you already did your detention for that,' Zoe said. 'Why does she need to see you again?'

Grace laughed nervously. 'Oh, you know Monty. Always loves a lecture.'

'But—' Zoe started.

'Zoe, just leave it—it's nothing!' Grace snapped.

We all went silent. It wasn't like Grace to be snappy. Zoe turned away, looking hurt.

'Grace, Zoe was only asking,' I said quietly.

'Yeah, well I already told you, so stop bugging me about it,' Grace said sharply.

What is going on with her?!

The bell pierced through the silence.

'Let's get to class,' Violet said hurriedly. She gathered up her rubbish and stood up, dusting off her dress. She reached out to help Grace up but Grace waved her hand dismissively and stood up herself.

'We've got art now,' I said with a smile, trying to break the tension.

'You go ahead, I'll catch up . . . later,' Grace said. She turned quickly and walked in the opposite direction.

'That was weird,' Ariel said once Grace was gone.

'What's up with her?' I asked. 'Grace is never like that.'

'She was rude,' Zoe huffed, clearly still offended by Grace's snappiness.

'I'm sure it's nothing,' Violet said. 'Let's just get to class and we can sort it out with her later.'

We all nodded and linked our arms together to walk through the school to our lockers. We needed to get our books for the next two lessons.

I added a little more blue paint to the green I was making, stirring the yellow and blue shades together until they swirled into an intoxicating green. I lifted my brush to the canvas and did a long stroke down the feather of the peacock I was painting.

'That's coming together beautifully, Ella,' Mrs Hodges said, approvingly.

I smiled gratefully as I turned back to my work. We were studying the idea of surrealism, which uses a strange mix of fact and fiction to create something new and usually bizarre. We'd looked at famous artists who painted things like melting clocks and dogs dressed in uniforms. Our task was to choose an animal and then put it in a strange environment that it didn't belong in. I decided to paint a bright peacock with its ornate feathers fanned outwards, standing in the middle of a drifting iceberg.

'Grace is still not here,' Zoe said, looking at her empty seat at our table. 'She's been gone half the lesson.'

'Maybe she's having her chat with Monty now?' Violet suggested.

'But she's been gone for, like, half an hour. That's a long chat,' Zoe said.

Ariel shrugged and continued painting her lion who was laying on the branch of a tall tree in a rainforest.

'I'm sure it's nothing,' I said, wiping a wisp of hair from my forehead with the back of my wrist so I wouldn't get paint on my face. 'Grace would tell us if something was up. We're best friends, after all.'

At that moment, Grace came into the art room. She walked over to Mrs Hodges and gave her a note. Mrs Hodges nodded and patted her on the back, then directed her over to her seat.

'That must have been quite the telling-off,' Violet said playfully.

'Huh?' Grace asked.

'Monty. Telling you off about the hat in the tree,' Violet reminded her.

'Oh, yeah, that. Yeah, she was going on and on about it. Never ended!' Grace laughed nervously. 'So, what'd I miss?'

Zoe looked at me with knowing eyes.

'Just continuing our paintings,' Zoe said flatly. I could tell she was still a bit annoyed at Grace for snapping at her earlier.

Grace walked over to the storeroom and came back out with her canvas. She turned it around and placed it on a table easel next to mine. Grace's artwork was amazing, as it always was. Turns out, Grace is an unbelievable artist. She even won a prize to take one of her artworks to London last term! Her painting depicted an orange orangutan sitting in the middle of a busy city scene. It looked like the centre of New York City on a particularly busy day. The orangutan was looking out to the viewer with sad eyes.

'Hey, Grace,' Ariel said, 'do you want to come with us down to the stables this afternoon? We're going to visit Zoe and Ella's horses.'

'Oh, no that's OK. I'm kinda behind on this artwork, so I might come back here to the art room later to do some more,' she replied. She focused her eyes on her painting and squinted at it.

'OK,' Ariel said, with a hint of confusion in her voice.

Grace seemed to paint in a frenzy over the next little while, trying to catch up on the part of the lesson that she'd missed.

'Girls, the bell will go in five minutes, so you need to start packing up,' Mrs Hodges said.

We took our brushes and paints over to the big metal sink and began to wash our things. Once done, I pulled off my smock and took my canvas over to the drying area. I returned to my table to collect my books just as the bell for the end of the lesson sounded.

Grace jumped. 'Oh, what?' she said. 'I haven't packed up!'

'Mrs Hodges told us five minutes ago,' I laughed. Classic Grace, not hearing the instructions.

'I didn't hear her,' she said, irritated.

'Grace, are you . . . are you OK?' I asked lightly, putting my hand on her shoulder.

She turned and smiled at me. 'Yes, of course, Ella. I'm fine. Honestly. I just need to wash up. You go—I don't want you to be late.'

I nodded and walked over to the artroom doorway.

Before leaving, I turned back to glance at Grace. She was washing her paintbrushes, swirls of orange and black paint cascading into the water. And for just a moment, I thought I saw a tear roll down her cheek.

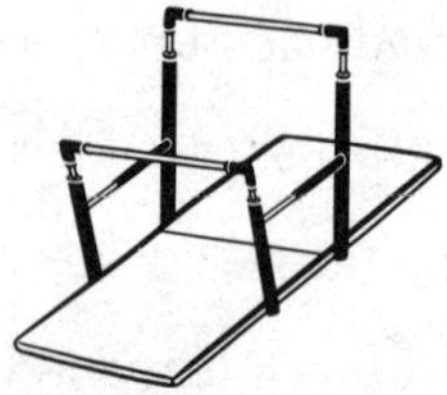

Chapter 5

I knocked on the door and waited. The door swung open and Mia greeted me with a smile.

'Hi, Ella. Come in,' she said, swinging the door open wider.

I walked inside and slipped my shoes off, leaving them near the front door. On a hallstand was a photo of Mia and Coach Marie—her mum—at a gym competition. Mia was smiling with medals slung around her neck. Coach Marie had an arm around her daughter and beamed at the camera.

I followed Mia down the hallway and into the living

area, which was adjoined to an open-plan kitchen. It was actually quite strange to be in a home. I was so used to being in the dorms or classrooms or other rooms at Eden College. The only time I was in a proper family house was when I went back home during the holidays. But Mia's family home sat on Eden campus near a cluster of other houses that housed other staff who lived on-site.

'Drink?' Mia offered, opening the fridge to gesture at the drinks on offer.

'Apple juice, please,' I said.

She poured us both a glass and I drank mine down thirstily. It had been a long and hot end to the school week and I was parched. That means very thirsty.

'Wanna go outside and do some gym tricks?' she asked.

I nodded.

I hadn't hung out with Mia at her house before, but she had invited me over. Her backyard was small but big enough to hold a trampoline with a net around it. For a moment, my heart ached. It looked like my trampoline from back home. And this suburban house and garden made me pine for my own family.

'You coming?' Mia asked as she climbed up onto the trampoline.

I shook away my memories of home and followed her up onto the trampoline, zipping up the net behind me.

Mia and I bounced in alternating rhythms.

'Wanna see my twists?' Mia said.

'Oh, yeah, show me,' I said, moving to the side of the trampoline. I leant against the netting to give her enough space to bounce.

Mia jumped higher and higher, circling her arms each time she went up into the air. Then she did a back layout (which is like a backward somersault in the air except your body is straight, not tucked up in a ball). As she reached full height, she pulled one of her arms in hard, making her body twist through the air. She landed and bounced onto her bottom, losing her balance.

'Cool!' I gasped. Coach Marie hardly ever let us muck around on the trampoline in the school gym.

'Your turn,' Mia said, moving to the side.

'How about a back pike?' I suggested.

She nodded.

I started to jump, bouncing higher and higher until I was high enough to do a backward pike, which is a backward somersault with straight legs and your body is bent in half.

'Sweet,' Mia said.

'So, how do you feel about training with boys?' I said, making a face like I'd swallowed something bitter.

'Ew ew ew!' Mia said, scrunching up her face.

'Why would your mum put us through that?' I asked dramatically.

'She's really good friends with the coach there—Coach Matt. He heads up the gym. They have worked together for years and are really close. I've known him since I was little. I bet it was his idea,' she said, rolling her eyes.

'Your turn,' I said. 'Try the twist again.'

Mia bounced once, then twice, then three times. When she was right up the top of her third jump, she arched backwards into a layout and pulled her arm in to twist. She almost got the whole way around but stopped short and fell on her bottom again.

'You're twisting too late,' a voice said from the doorway to the house.

Mia grimaced.

'Hi, Coach Marie,' I said.

'Mum, you're not my coach here,' Mia reminded her. 'You're just my mum. Now hurry along,' Mia said, waving her hands to shoo her mum away. For a second I thought Coach Marie looked a bit hurt.

'I'll make you girls something to eat,' she said.

'No, it's OK—' Mia began, but Coach Marie had already gone back inside.

'How cool to have a coach for a mum,' I said. 'Does she teach you cool stuff at home? I'd love it if my mum could spot me for new things.'

'Yeah, it sounds fun,' Mia said. But it's all gym-gym-gym. It gets super boring.'

We hopped off the trampoline and went inside. I was instantly hit with the delicious smell of popcorn.

'Here you go, girls,' Coach Marie said, putting a steaming bowl down at the table.

'I think we'll eat in my room, if that's OK,' Mia said.

Coach Marie hesitated then said, 'Of course.'

I gave her a little wave as we turned to go to Mia's room.

'Ella, are you staying for dinner? Do you need me to let Ms Montgomery know you are going to eat here tonight?' Coach Marie said. 'I can do Bolognese or chicken burgers or—'

'Actually, I'm going to the dorms tonight,' Mia interrupted.

'Oh, again?' Coach Marie asked.

I stood awkwardly between them, tension thick in the air.

'Yeah, it's movie night and I'm allowed over there for movie night. And Ms Montgomery said I'm welcome there for dinner any time I want, as long as you are OK with it,' Mia said. She narrowed her eyes, assessing her mum's face.

'Oh, right. But I thought tonight we were going to catch up on our show,' she said.

'We can watch that any time,' Mia said dismissively.

'And anyhow, it's getting a little boring.'

'Which show?' I asked.

'*Perfect Score*,' Mia said. 'You know, the gymnastics one?'

'Yeah, I've seen it—it's good!' I said.

'I thought you loved gymnastics shows,' Coach Marie said, frowning.

'I'm a bit sick of them,' Mia said, shrugging.

Coach Marie's cheeks went pink. She nodded and smiled. 'Of course you can go to the dorm later. Have fun.'

We left Coach Marie in the kitchen and walked up the hallway towards the front of the house. I looked to one side into what was obviously Coach Marie's bedroom. Then I looked into the next room. It was set up with a bed, a bookshelf full of books, a desk, fairy lights and a bean bag.

'Whose room is that?' I asked.

'Oh, it's the spare room,' Mia said hurriedly.

'But it's decorated for a girl,' I said.

Mia shrugged. 'Just me and mum here,' she said.

I let it go and followed her into her room.

'I'll change and then we can go,' she said.

'We've got heaps of time before dinner though,' I said. 'I'm happy to hang here.'

Mia shook her head. 'Let's just go hang at the dorm. It's more fun.'

I nodded. But as I turned to look back up the hallway, I briefly glimpsed Coach Marie sink into her couch seat and put her head in her hands.

Chapter 6

'Ella, sit with me,' Mia said, patting the seat next to her.

I plonked my gym bag onto the floor of the minibus and sat down beside her. Charlotte and Jasmine were sitting behind us. We did up our seat belts as Coach Marie climbed into the driver's seat and started the engine.

'How long's the drive?' Mia asked her mum.

'Not long at all—about an hour to the coast,' Coach Marie replied as she adjusted the rear view mirror.

'What's the gym like?' I asked the others. As the only Year 7 in the team, I had never competed in an

Interschools Championship before, and I had never been to the Southern Beaches gym either. I'd been in other competitions with my gymnastics club in primary school, but this one was different. Everyone attending this championship was competing for their school. This would be my first time representing Eden College.

'It's massive,' Jasmine replied. 'They have like, six sets of bars, multiple beams, a massive sprung floor and a giant foam pit.'

'Awesome,' I said, smiling. The old gym that I used to go to in primary school had a foam pit. A foam pit is basically a giant hole in the floor that is filled with soft foam cubes. It's super fun to jump into and it provides a soft landing, a bit like a ball pit in a kids' play centre. When I used to practice a new and scary skill, it really helped with my confidence to know I would be landing somewhere softer than the standard floor mats. It was also awesome fun when we set up a metal bar above the pit and we could do massive swings off it into the soft foam below—it was like landing in a giant pool of clouds!

After we'd been driving for half an hour, I could see the ocean quietly peeking out at us from the front windscreen.

'I see the ocean!' I yelled excitedly.

A beautiful, white sandy beach came into view. The sunlight danced on top of the water and I could almost smell the salty air, even from inside the minibus. We curled through some quiet backstreets until we turned into a large carpark that sat in front of a big building that looked like a warehouse. On top of the building there was a sign, 'Southern Beaches Gymnastics Academy—building the stars of tomorrow'.

We pulled into a parking spot and Coach Marie hopped out to open the door of the minibus. I stepped out and breathed in the fresh salty beach air. Even though we were less than an hour from Eden College, the air smelled completely different. The bushy scent of eucalyptus was replaced by the scent of seaweed, ocean and sunscreen. I breathed it in deeply. It reminded me of our beach holidays with my grandparents where they would take us fishing on the wharf.

We walked into the building and the fresh smells of the ocean were immediately replaced by the familiar scent of gymnastics. It's a hard thing to describe, but to me, it felt like coming home. Just like our gym at Eden, gymnasts were everywhere, stretching, tumbling and doing strength exercises. I looked up to the ceiling and there was a long rope hanging down. A boy was using his arms to climb towards the top of the rope. He must have climbed all the way up there without even using his legs! He cheered as he made it to the top. I glanced at Mia with wide eyes.

We put our gym bags in the cubby holes on the side of the gym and removed our shoes and tracksuits. We were allowed to train in any leotards we liked, which weren't the same as our special competition leotards.

I was wearing a black leotard with little diamond sparkles all over it. It was sleeveless and had ornate criss-cross straps across the back. I pulled on my black velvet bike pants and twisted my hair into a high bun.

Mia's leotard was bright pink and purple with swirls on the front. She fiddled with her hair nervously as she watched the boys climb up and down the ropes with ease.

'Girls, over here, please,' Coach Marie said, gesturing for us to come over to the floor mats.

She was standing next to a tall man with dark hair and almond eyes. He smiled warmly as us.

'This is my friend, Coach Matt,' Coach Marie said.

We smiled and waved shyly.

'Coach Matt and I have trained gymnasts together for many years. He coaches the boys' program here and I think he might have some good tips for you girls,' Coach Marie said.

'And in return,' Coach Matt said, smiling, 'I hope that Coach Marie and you girls might have some helpful things to share with my squad.'

Coach Matt then whistled sharply, and the boys on the ropes climbed down and ran over to us on the mats. I counted seven in total, which was almost double our squad.

'Boys,' Coach Matt said, 'here are the gymnasts from Eden College I told you about. Can you please introduce yourselves?'

The previously rambunctious boys suddenly looked shy. Coach Matt laughed. 'I think this is the first time my boys here have been silent! OK, I'll introduce you then. This is my Level 5 squad.' Coach Matt then walked along the line of boys, placing his hand on each shoulder as he introduced their names. 'We have Ravi, Iggy, James, Blake, Michael and our twins, Bowen and Rowan.'

The boys waved. Coach Marie then introduced us, smiling proudly as she called each of our names. We gave a small wave back.

'Boys, continue with your strength work on the ropes while the girls warm up. Then later we can get some challenges going,' Coach Matt said, winking at us.

The boys ran off and left us to warm up.

'Start with a jog around the mats,' Coach Marie said. 'Followed by tuck jumps, chassés and punch jumps. Then start your stretching.'

Coach Marie went to talk to some of the Southern Beaches gym staff while we warmed ourselves up. We'd done the warm up routine a million times before and didn't need any prompting to know what to do.

Once we'd done the energetic part of the warm up, we started to stretch. I slid down into slide splits, wincing ever so slightly, and held the stretch with the others. We always talked while we stretched—it took our minds off the discomfort.

'What do you think of the boys' squad?' Charlotte asked.

'There's a lot of them,' Jasmine said, looking over to the group of boys.

'They look pretty strong, too,' I said, glancing over. They had now moved to the parallel bars and were doing impressive swings and handstands on top of the bars.

'Yeah, well, I'd like to see them try a cartwheel on beam,' Mia said, grinning. We all knew boy gymnasts didn't compete on beam as an apparatus.

I moved into front splits and held it, breathing through the stretch.

'Nearly warmed up?' a voice said from behind. I turned and saw Coach Marie standing there.

'Yes,' we chorused.

'Good, because we have your first challenge,' Coach

Marie said, smiling.

My tummy flipped nervously.

'We're going to have a tumbling competition against the boys!' she declared.

Jasmine, Charlotte, Mia and I smiled at each other. We were pretty good tumblers and would surely give those boys a run for their money.

We walked over to the tumble track, which is a very long, air-inflated mat that is bouncy. Not as bouncy as a trampoline, but bouncy enough to get some pretty good height off it when you hit it hard.

Four members of the boys' squad came over and lined up by the tumble track, ready for the challenge.

'OK, tumbling challenge is ready to go!' Coach Matt smiled. 'I'll give you a skill. You each perform the skill and will get a point every time you stick it.'

We called this game 'stick it' and played it all the time in our own gym.

'We'll start easy,' Coach Matt said. 'Front handspring.'

We all nodded.

Charlotte went first and did a neat handspring.

She rebounded into the air, stuck her landing and then presented her arms.

'One point!' Coach Matt declared.

Next, the boy named Ravi had a go. He stuck his landing easily and his squad cheered for him.

Jasmine had a turn, but after her rebound, she wobbled forwards and took a big step out of her landing.

It was then Blake's turn and he stuck his landing too.

'Two to one, to the boys!' Coach Marie called.

Now it was my turn. I ran and launched myself into a front handspring. I rebounded high and my body tipped forwards. I took a big step, stumbled and landed on my knees. My cheeks flamed with embarrassment.

'Unlucky, Ella,' Coach Marie said.

'Let's make it harder,' Coach Matt said. 'Bowen, front tuck.'

Bowen ran fast down the tumble track. He punched off two feet and tucked his body into a front somersault. He opened out and landed on his feet, like they were stuck in cement.

The boys' squad cheered loudly.

'Three to one to the boys,' Coach Matt said.

Mia took her turn. Running down the track, she performed a high front somersault. She stuck it perfectly and her mum beamed.

'Three to two to the boys!' Coach Marie called.

Iggy, the last to go, launched himself into a front somersault with ease. But his balance wavered at the end and he stepped forward slightly.

'Unlucky, dude,' Bowen said, clapping Iggy on the back.

We continued the game into another round, and Jasmine, Charlotte and I all stuck our landings. Mia stuck her roundoff backflip and back somersault. The boys all stuck their landings, too.

'Ooh, it's going to be tight!' Coach Matt said. 'Seven to the boys, six to the girls.'

'How about double or nothing?' Mia called out in a confident voice. 'If the next person does a skill with a twist and sticks it, we get double points.'

Coach Matt looked at Coach Marie. 'I like it!' he said.

Both teams huddled together to work out which

gymnast they wanted to put forward for the last double or nothing round.

'Mia, you've got this,' I said. 'You're the best at twisting—do a roundoff, back handspring, back layout with a half twist.'

Charlotte and Jasmine agreed.

Mia nodded firmly.

The boys nominated Ravi to do a twisting tumbling row. He did a roundoff back handspring, then added a back somersault with a half twist. But he landed short and put his hands on the ground for balance.

'Dang!' he cursed as he walked back to his squad.

'Go Mia!' Charlotte cheered.

Mia focused on the tumble track, blocking out the noise around her. She frowned resolutely, then thundered down the track. She did her roundoff back handspring perfectly, then performed a soaring layout, which is like a back somersault but with a straight body in the air. She pulled one arm in so her body twisted, then she landed facing down the mat. Her feet stuck to the mat like glue, and she threw her arms out to finish in a final 'present'.

'WOOHOO!' Charlotte, Jasmine and I cheered, running down the mats to hug Mia.

'Girls rule!' Jasmine sang.

The boys looked annoyed but then smiled and came down to shake our hands. They were good sports.

'You rule, Mia,' Jasmine said, giving her a hug. 'You just have to bring that game to the Interschools comp!'

'Oh, I will,' Mia said smiling. For a moment, a slight frown crossed her face, but she shook her head and plastered on a smile.

Chapter 7

I slid across the bench seat until I was next to Zoe. I mixed my yoghurt and cereal together and took a quick sip of juice.

'More gym training this week?' Zoe asked, taking a bite of her toast.

'Mmmhmm,' I mumbled as I swallowed a mouthful of muesli. 'So much training. We have all these additional sessions in the lead up to Interschools. I'm super excited about the comp but also really nervous. It's my first big competition for Eden College.'

'You'll be great,' Zoe smiled.

‘I just need to remember not to stack it on beam,’ I said. I got frustrated just thinking about the back walkover on the high beam.

‘You gymnasts are so *messy*,’ a snide voice said from the other side of the table.

Saskia.

‘Saskia, you *are* a gymnast,’ Zoe said, scrunching up her face.

‘Ugh, not like *that*,’ Saskia said, disgusted. ‘I am a rhythmic gymnast. You know, the ones with the ball, hoop and beautiful ribbons—you must have seen them in the Olympics.’

‘Sure,’ Zoe said, not overly interested.

‘We are the ballerinas of the gymnastics world,’ Saskia said in a lofty voice. ‘We embody grace, flexibility and beauty. Something those artistic gymnasts like Ella know nothing about!’

‘Artistic gymnasts are graceful!’ I said, annoyed.

‘Running up the vault mat like a freight train? I don’t think so,’ Saskia scoffed.

I rolled my eyes and focused on my cereal.

'Hey, there's Violet!' Zoe said, looking towards the dining hall door. Zoe waved her over to us.

We watched as Violet picked up her diabetic-friendly breakfast and came over.

'Where are Grace and Ariel?' I asked her.

'They were at the nurse taking their morning medicine with me,' Violet said. 'They should be here soon.'

Anyone who needed special medications in the morning had to go to the nurse to get it. Violet went up to manage her diabetes and Ariel had to go each morning for her asthma puffer. But Grace didn't need medicine.

'Why was Grace there? She doesn't have daily medication,' I said, frowning.

'I thought that, too,' Violet said. 'She looked like she was totally hiding from me in the line. But when I went up to her she said she just had a headache.'

I shrugged.

Grace and Ariel then walked into the dining hall and picked up their breakfasts. They wandered over to us and sat down.

'Your head OK?' I asked Grace.

'My head?' she asked, confused.

'Your headache. Violet said you had a headache.'

Grace's face registered and she waved her hand dismissively. 'Oh, yeah, that. All good now. Must have just slept funny on my neck!'

Grace smiled and started eating her breakfast quickly. I glanced at Zoe, but she didn't seem to sense anything weird, so I kept eating. I couldn't help but watch Grace as she ate. She had a little frown on her face and I could feel her tension.

Nanna Kate says I am an intuitive person. She says that means I notice the really little things that most people don't—that I'm good at knowing what people feel by little things they do, or by looks that they give. And at that moment, my intuition was telling me that Grace wasn't quite herself. And she wasn't telling us why.

'Do you know what we haven't done in ages?' I said in a cheerful voice. 'A DRMF!'

Grace's face brightened as she looked up. DRMF is our code for Dorm Room Midnight Feast. We'd done a couple before but it usually ended up with us getting into massive trouble, or narrowly avoiding trouble by the skin of our teeth. But it was always so much fun and it was just the thing Grace needed to cheer her up from whatever was going on.

'YES!' Ariel said excitedly. Ariel had only joined the school last term after travelling around for years as a movie star. She'd never really done normal-kid stuff like sleepovers, midnight feasts or parties.

'Ooh, did I hear Midnight Feast?' Saskia said, leaning in with a smile.

I rolled my eyes.

'Yeah, wanna come?' Grace asked brightly.

If there was one super-power Grace had, it was the power of inclusion. She never seemed to have issues with anyone, and was always happy to invite everyone along to everything. Even though I didn't really want Saskia there, I knew Grace was doing the right thing by being kind.

'Whose room?' Mercedes asked from next to Saskia.

'Ours,' I said, since I had come up with the idea in

the first place.

'See you tonight!' Portia said from Saskia's other side.

Portia, Saskia, Mercedes and Ariel were all in a dorm together, so it made sense they all came along.

Grace looked up at me and smiled gratefully. She didn't have to say it with words, because I already knew she was saying thank you.

That night, Grace, Zoe and I set up our pillows and blankets on the floor, ready for our DRMF. Grace pulled out her latest haul of candy from her dad's business trip to America, which he always had sent to us in secret packages so that Ms Montgomery didn't confiscate them.

'What's a Snickerdoodle?!' Zoe laughed, picking up one of the chocolates.

Suddenly, there was a rhythmic tap on the door. We froze, listening for the secret code in the knock.

'The knock has to be to the rhythm of 'Love Story' by Taylor Swift. I'm pretty sure that's 'Shake It Off',' Grace said, tilting her head to the side.

'Either way, it's obviously not Monty,' I laughed, standing up to open the door a crack.

Ariel, Saskia, Mercedes and Portia were huddled together in the hallway, glancing nervously up and down the hallway in case Ms Montgomery was on the prowl.

'Quick, let us in!' Saskia hissed.

We let them in and everyone gathered together on the carpet in a circle, with the candy in the centre.

'I hereby—' Saskia started.

'Hey!' I interrupted. 'This DRMF was my idea. I'm the president tonight!'

Saskia rolled her eyes and folded her arms across her chest.

I cleared my voice. 'I hereby declare this DRMF meeting open!'

We all dived into the centre of the circle to take a piece of candy each. Violet stood up and opened her drawer, pulling out her own special treats that were OK for her to eat.

'Not much candy tonight,' Zoe said, frowning.

It was true. The centre of the circle was already

empty and we'd only had one each.

'Sorry, my dad isn't due on another business trip until next month,' Grace said. 'That's all I've got!'

'Anyone got anything else? Maybe from a trip to the shops?' Mercedes asked hopefully.

We all shook our heads.

'I know!' Saskia said, brightening. 'We have those yummy chocolate biscuits in the kitchenette downstairs! Remember the ones Monty bought as a treat for Movie Night?'

The dorm room had a small kitchenette in it for making tea and hot chocolate or popcorn in the microwave. It wasn't a big kitchen like the one in the dining hall.

'Do you think she kept the spares in the kitchenette?' Portia asked.

'Only one way to find out!' Grace giggled mischievously.

'Who's going to sneak to the kitchenette and get it? It's right next door to Monty's room,' Ariel said.

'I did the last dare,' I said, folding my arms.

'Remember when Ariel and I were dared to sneak out and we got stuck outside Mrs Sinclair's bedroom window?!'

'Maybe we draw straws,' Violet suggested, standing up.

'I'm good at drawing!' Grace said brightly.

'No, not that kind of drawing,' Violet giggled. 'I'll hold a bunch of pencils in my hand, each different lengths. But you won't be able to see how long each one is because only the tops will be visible and I'll make sure they look the same. Whoever picks the smallest two pencils will have to go.'

We all nodded in agreement.

Violet trotted over to the desk and pulled out a stack of pencils. She held them in her fist so that the lead tip of the pencil was covered in her hand, but the rubber ends all stood out at the same height. She offered them around to each of us.

Once we each had a pencil, we laid them all out on the carpet to see who had the shortest ones.

'Oh, dang!' Saskia cursed, looking at her tiny pencil.

We lined the others up.

'I think it's me,' Zoe said, annoyed.

'No, it's Ella,' Violet said, pointing at my pencil.

I held my pencil up against Zoe's and mine was definitely shorter.

Blergh.

'Fine. Ella and I can do it, right Ella?' Saskia said.

I sighed. 'Here we go again!'

Saskia and I stood up and crept to the door. I gently pulled it open, being careful not to make it squeak. I gestured with my hand for Saskia to follow me.

We slowly tiptoed to the top of the stairs and gently descended, one by one. Every time a step creaked, we froze like deer in headlights.

As I got to the bottom of the stairs, Ms Montgomery's door came into view. It was closed.

We stealthily crept up the hallway, past the lounge and towards the small kitchen at the back of the dorm house. We stumbled through the door and into a room dimly lit by a full moon.

'We made it!' Saskia whispered excitedly. 'Pull the

door closed a bit so nobody hears us rummaging around.'

I gently pulled the door until it was only slightly ajar.

'Check the cupboards over there,' I said, pointing under the microwave. 'I'll check these ones.'

I opened a cupboard and started rifling through, but could only find boring crackers, teabags and cleaning supplies.

Then we heard it.

Creeeak!

'What was that?' Saskia hissed.

We shuffled over to the door and listened again.

Creeeak! Creeeeak!

'Someone's coming!' I whispered. 'Hide!'

We ran over to the other side of the kitchen, stumbling in the dimly-lit room. Saskia leapt into the tall broom cupboard and pulled the door until only a small crack remained.

I looked around the room wildly, trying desperately to find a place to hide. The cupboards were all too small.

I looked down and saw that the centre counter didn't sit flush on the ground. It stood on small metal feet, leaving a very narrow space underneath. As the footsteps got closer, instinct kicked in and my body did what it knew best. I slid down into the side-splits, with my tummy lying on the ground in a pancake stretch. Then I used my arms to push my flattened body underneath the counter.

Light footsteps stopped just outside the door. Then they padded into the kitchen. I could see two pairs of feet in soft slippers. *Teacher slippers or girl slippers?*

The feet shuffled over to the far side of the kitchen and I heard one of the cabinets open. And then a giggle. That sure didn't sound like Ms Montgomery.

Saskia must have had the very same thought, because at that moment she burst out from the broom cupboard and hit the lights. Brightness flooded the room, stabbing at our eyes. I slid out from under the counter.

'What are you doing?' Saskia hissed.

'AAAAAAGGGH!'

The two visitors startled, and a jar of chocolate biscuits dropped from their hands. It fell loudly to the floor, and biscuits tumbled out everywhere.

'Ella! Saskia!' Charlotte cried out, holding her hand to her chest.

'You scared us to death!' Jasmine hissed.

It was my two gym friends, Charlotte and Jasmine.

'Stealing biscuits, hey?' Saskia said accusingly.

'Yeah, and what are you two doing in here then?' Charlotte said with narrow eyes.

'At least you found them,' I said, giggling. 'We weren't so lucky.'

There was a light thud and a shuffling sound coming from the hallway.

'You woke Monty!' Saskia whispered.

'It's your fault for scaring us!' Jasmine said, as she looked around for somewhere to hide.

Saskia rolled her eyes and pulled Jasmine into the broom cupboard with her. I slid back down into my side-splits and pushed my body along the ground until I was underneath the counter. Charlotte followed, just squeezing in beside me. Lucky gymnasts are so bendy!

The door flung open and I could see the unmistakable pattern of Ms Montgomery's slippers.

'Who is in here?' she said in a stern voice. 'Come out now and you'll be in less trouble.'

We held our breath.

She saw the empty jar and began to pick up the scattered biscuits. Then I saw her opening cupboards, looking for the culprit. She was only centimetres away from the broom cupboard. Jasmine and Saskia were doomed!

'Oh no,' Charlotte breathed.

Meow.

Ms Montgomery's cat, Crystal, suddenly jumped up onto the counter and meowed again. She must have snuck in through the open door without us noticing.

'Did you knock over this jar, you naughty girl?' Ms Montgomery said, picking up her cat. She tutted then walked over to the door, satisfied that she'd found the culprit. She flicked off the light switch and walked back up the hallway.

'That was close,' Jasmine said, slipping out of the cupboard.

'We'd better get back to our beds. I bet Monty will

check in on everyone once she settles Crystal back in her room,' Charlotte said, heading for the door.

Just before we left the room I jogged back over to the pile of biscuits on the counter and stuffed a few in my gown pocket.

'Ella, really?' Saskia hissed.

I shrugged. 'Can't go back empty handed, right?'

Saskia shook her head as Charlotte and Jasmine laughed silently into their hands.

Chapter 8

× –

From: Ella

Sent: Saturday 7:47 AM

To: Olivia

Subject: Off to training

Hi Olivia,

Just a quick email this morning. We have training at Southern Beaches gym again today. Coach Marie said we're going to have a strength competition against the boys. I'm a bit nervous—I've seen them train and they are soooo strong! But we are also strong, so I'm hoping we win. Coach Marie said we need to focus on getting past our mental blocks. That's a fancy phrase we use in sports for when you feel like you can't do something because your mind keeps saying you can't, even if you can. My mental block is the back walkover on beam. For Mia, it's vault. So I have to sort that out before the Interschools comp in two weeks. Blergh. Do you get this with soccer? Probably not! I think it's a bit of a gymnastics thing.

Oh, and when I call you later, remind me to tell you about the funniest DRMF ever the other night!

Thanks for trying to think of what might be going on with Grace. She said she's definitely not homesick, so that isn't it. Keep thinking!

Love, Ella.

After arriving at Southern Beaches gym, we put our gear in the cubbies and began our warm up. We started with some light jogging up and down the mats, followed by jumping, sashaying, and leaps. We did rows of handstands, cartwheels and walkovers, and finished off with a long stretch to get our muscles nice and supple. That means bendy, by the way.

We could see the boys training on the other side of the gym, practicing circle skills on the pommel horse. The pommel horse isn't used in women's gymnastics, which I am kind of glad about because it looks super-duper hard to circle around and around like that with only your hands for balance.

'Those boys must have strong wrists,' Jasmine said, as if reading my thoughts.

'Girls, straight to vault,' an unfamiliar voice called from behind us.

It was a coach we hadn't seen before, leading a small team of girls into the gym. They had probably come from another part of the gym where they would have done their own stretching and strength training. The four girls eyed us suspiciously as they walked towards the vault.

'That's our competition,' Mia said, matter-of-factly.

I wasn't familiar with any of the other clubs

competing at Interschools, since I'd never represented Eden College in gymnastics before. But Mia, Jasmine and Charlotte had, so they recognised the girls immediately.

'They are the Level 6 gymnasts from this club,' Jasmine said. 'Everyone at this club goes to either Southern Beaches Girls' School or Southern Beaches Boys' School. They are really good. Especially that smaller girl—they call her the pocket-rocket. She's tiny but she's really good. Her name is Alexa.'

I watched as Alexa thundered down the mat towards the vault. She hit the vault with force and went sailing over it through a handstand that popped right off the vault, sending her flying through the air. Then she landed perfectly on her two feet.

Mia winced.

'She won the all-rounder for Level 5 last year,' Charlotte added.

'I actually beat her on every apparatus,' Mia said, sounding annoyed. 'All except vault. Our scores were super close and I was leading on bars, beam and floor.

But then I stuffed up my vault and she scored a 9.6, which meant she won overall. I didn't even place.'

Mia shook her head, apparently still angry at herself for a competition from nearly a year ago.

'Well, maybe this year is your turn,' I said, trying to comfort her.

She muttered to herself and shook her head slightly.

We watched as the Southern Beaches girls stuck vault after vault, sailing over the table with ease. They were all really good.

Coach Marie wandered over and saw us gazing at the Southern Beaches gymnasts.

'You know,' she started slowly, 'it's better to be inspired to beat the competition, not feel intimidated by it.'

'They are so good,' I said, biting my lip.

'You girls are just as good. Sure, you might need to work on one or two things, but I believe you can beat them!' Coach Marie said, eyeing Mia.

Mia rolled her eyes.

'But we're not thinking about that right now,' Coach Marie continued. 'First, we have to focus on beating someone *else* from this club.' Her eyes twinkled with mischief as Coach Matt led his team of boys over to where we were standing.

'Oh no, not the boys!' Mia moaned.

'Thanks for the warm welcome,' Coach Matt laughed sarcastically as he heard Mia's protest.

'It's time for a strength challenge,' Coach Marie said. 'Are you girls game?'

Jasmine and Charlotte perked up. 'Game on!' Charlotte hollered.

The boys in the team smirked.

'Let's start with rope climbs,' Coach Matt said.

I looked at Jasmine and Charlotte who nodded confidently. Mia brightened slightly—she was an excellent rope climber.

'Let's do this!' Mia said, standing up.

We all walked to the two long hanging ropes which were attached to the high ceiling of the gym. It was a long way up and I felt my tummy flip and flop.

'Relay race,' Coach Matt said. 'Climb to the top, touch the roof, then climb back down. Notice I said *climb* down, not drop. Once you get to the ground, tag the next person to go.'

'Easy!' Jasmine said, smiling ruefully.

'Too easy!' one of the boys added.

'Uh, uh, ah!' Coach Marie interrupted. 'There's one more bit. You can't use your legs to climb. You have to have your legs pointing outwards in a pike hold the entire time.'

I could feel my stomach and arm muscles aching already at the thought of such a long climb using only my arms.

'Boys, who wants to compete in this challenge?' Coach Matt asked his squad.

The twins, Bowen and Rowan, jumped up and down with their hands in the air.

'OK, twins, you're up. And, let me see, Blake and Iggy,' Coach Matt said.

The four boys huddled together to make a game plan. So we did, too.

'Ella, you are zippy so you should go first to try and get us a head start. Then maybe me, then Jasmine.

Then I think Mia should go last because she's the strongest,' Charlotte said.

We all nodded and lined up in front of the ropes.

'Take your mark, get set, GO!'

I jumped up and grabbed the rope with my hands. I pointed my legs out straight in front of me and squeezed them tight to hold their position. Then I began the long ascent, hand over hand.

I glanced next to me where one of the twins was shimmying up the rope like a rat up a drainpipe. I could already see he was ahead of me.

'Ella, focus on your own climb,' Coach Marie yelled, seeing me eye off the competition.

'You can do it!' Jasmine encouraged.

I frowned and focused on my climb. Coach Marie was right, I didn't need to watch the boy next to me. I needed to worry about myself. I could see the muscles in my arm bulge as I kept climbing, hand over hand. My stomach muscles began to ache as I neared the top. I desperately wanted to hook my feet onto the rope to give my arms a break. But I knew I couldn't.

I finally touched the roof, and from here at the top of the rope I could see across the entire gym. I glanced around and saw that the Southern Beaches girls had stopped their vaulting to watch us. I shook away the distraction and focused on my hands.

I began to descend the rope, still holding my legs out in front of me. The rules were that we couldn't just drop down. And sliding down a rope like a fireman's pole would just result in very serious rope burn. No, I had to climb down, one hand at a time.

The twin I was competing against, Rowan, was slightly slower on the way down. He must have used all of his energy to climb up the rope, as I could see his arms trembling as he descended.

I quickened my pace, gritting my teeth through the pain.

As I reached the bottom of the rope and my feet finally touched the ground, I saw that I had overtaken Rowan.

'Go, Ella!' my teamed cheered.

The whole gym had stopped to watch the race. I tagged Charlotte, who leapt up to the rope and began her climb. A few seconds into Charlotte's ascent, Rowan had reached the ground and tagged Iggy, who very quickly caught up to Charlotte. He was fast. By the time Charlotte was halfway down her climb, Iggy had jumped off and was tagging the next boy, Blake.

Jasmine climbed as fast as she could, hand over hand. But I could tell she was struggling. Arm strength wasn't Jasmine's best asset—she was a very graceful gymnast who was much better at floor and beam. By the time she'd finished her turn, the boys were way ahead, with the other twin scaling the rope well before Mia had even been tagged.

Jasmine tapped Mia and Mia sprang into action. Her legs pointed outwards, tight and straight. Her hands gripped the rope. She climbed at high speed, her arms working like machines. By the time the second twin had reached the top, Mia had caught up. She just had to keep up with him on the descent.

'Go, Bowen!' a voice screamed from the other side of the gym. I turned and saw the small girl from the other team, Alexa, running over and cheering for the

Southern Beaches boys.

'Beaches! Beaches!' she began to cheer. The rest of the gymnasts from the club joined in.

'Beaches! Beaches!'

Mia's eyes darted around the gym and she lost her concentration, focusing instead on the people cheering for the boy on the other rope.

'Come on, Mia!' I yelled, but my voice was drowned out by the throng of gymnasts from the Southern Beaches club.

'Beaches! Beaches!' they hollered.

Mia's focus was now on the crowd at the bottom of the rope. As she stared at Alexa, her hand missed the rope and her body jolted as she swung from the rope by one arm. Exhausted from her climb, she couldn't support her body with just one hand and she fell from the rope to the crash mat below. She wasn't very high up so her fall was soft and she landed on her bottom just as Bowen finished his climb. The gym erupted into cheers as he high-fived his team mates.

Mia sat on the mat in embarrassment, but was too

exhausted to get up.

'Good try, Mia,' Coach Marie said, extending her hand to help her up.

Mia ignored her mum's extended arm and stood on her own.

'OK, show's over,' Coach Matt said, smiling and gesturing for the other gymnasts to get back to their training.

The crowd dispersed.

'Don't worry, Mia, we'll get them next time,' Charlotte said gently.

'Poor Eden College. They never beat Southern Beaches,' a voice said behind us.

Alexa stood there with a sly grin on her face. 'I guess it's just tradition!' Alexa smirked as she walked away.

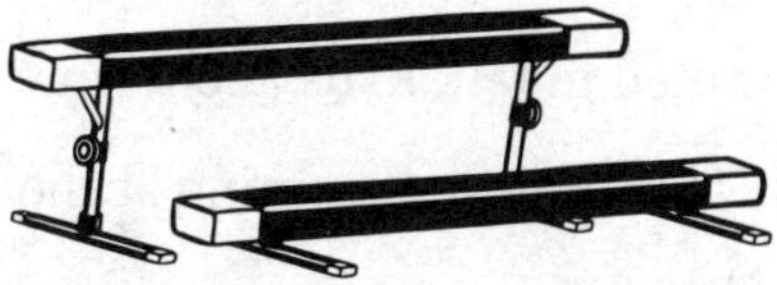

Chapter 9

The following Monday we were back in our own gym for training. Mia had been a little quiet since our Saturday session at Southern Beaches. I couldn't work out if it was losing the strength challenge to the boys or if Alexa was getting in her head. Usually Mia could shake stuff like that off, but as the Interschools competition got closer, her mood seemed to darken each day. Either way, I knew she was thinking about her vault. And I couldn't blame her. The closer the competition came, the more worried I became about my back walkover on the beam.

Coach Marie had instructed us to work on our most

troublesome apparatus this session. But before we got started, she wanted to talk to us about something.

'I hope you've all enjoyed training at the Southern Beaches gym. It's given you great experience before the comp,' she said.

We all nodded in agreement.

'Since the comp is now only two weeks away, I had a chat with the girls' coach at Southern Beaches and she agreed it would be good to have a bit of a practice competition with them this weekend. What do you think?' Coach Marie asked.

'Against Alexa and the other Level 6 girls?' Charlotte asked. 'They are so good though.'

'I think it's just the thing you need to motivate you before the competition. Might make some of you pick up your game a bit,' Coach Marie said, glancing quickly at Mia.

Mia rolled her eyes.

'Everyone off to work on your routines. I'll start with Charlotte and Ella on beam. Mia, go warm up with vault and Jasmine, you're on bars,' Coach Marie instructed.

I walked over to the beams and did some warm up drills with Charlotte. I then went through my routine on the high beam, including my mount, leaps and handstand. I left out the back walkover.

'Ella, come down to the low beam and warm up your back walkovers,' Coach Marie said.

She spotted me for the first few. Then I started to do some by myself.

'See? You've got this,' Coach Marie said, as I completed a back walkover on the lowest beam.

'Yeah, but this beam is like, 20 centimetres off the ground,' I protested.

'This is what's called a mental block, Ella,' Coach Marie said. 'There's no difference between the beams other than one being elevated. It's the same width. Same skill. Same movement. It's your brain telling you that you can't do it. But you can.'

I knew she was right. But sometimes my mind just wouldn't let me believe I could do something.

Coach Marie turned to scan the gym. 'Straight arms in that kip, Jasmine,' she called over to Jasmine on bars.

Her eyes then landed on Mia.

I followed her gaze towards the vaulting table. Mia took a fast run-up, then hit the board strongly with her feet. But her handspring over the vaulting table was slow and she didn't push through her hands into the air. She flopped over the table and landed on her feet on the other side, falling backwards onto her bottom.

'Pop those shoulders!' Coach Marie yelled.

'The vaulting table is too high,' Mia moaned.

'It's regulation height, Mia. I've trained six-year-olds who get over that thing,' Coach Marie said with irritation in her voice.

Mia stood up angrily and stomped back down the run-up.

'She'd be so good if she'd just listen,' Coach Marie mumbled under her breath.

I thought about saying something. Something about how we all have struggles and will get it right eventually. And that Mia wasn't doing it on purpose. But this wasn't just a coach and a gymnast. This was a mother and daughter. I didn't want to get in the middle of that.

'Up to the top beam, Ella,' Coach Marie said.

I began to shake my head.

'I'll spot you,' she promised, dragging a box over to the beam to stand on so she could support me through my walkover.

I nodded and stood on the high beam. I reached my arms tall and Coach Marie gently put one hand on the small of my back and the other behind my legs. I arched back and grasped the beam with my hands, then kicked over.

'There, see?' Coach Marie said. 'Again.'

'Promise to spot me?' I asked.

She nodded.

I did another walkover with Coach Marie gently guiding me through the movement. I wobbled at the end but she steadied me with her hand. I felt so much safer with her there.

'Again,' Coach Marie said. 'Over and over until it becomes second nature.'

'You have to spot again though,' I said, nervous that she might try to sneak away.

It reminded me of when I learned to ride a bike. Dad would run along behind me, holding the seat to keep me steady. He said he wouldn't let go, but then eventually he did, just to show me that I could do it by myself. But the second I realised he wasn't holding on, the handlebars began to wibble and wobble. I swerved from side to side before falling off sideways into a bush.

Coach Marie put a light hand on my back.

'You're spotting me, right?' I said.

'Yes, Ella. I'm not going to trick you.'

I nodded. But her fingertips felt lighter on my leotard than last time. I started to arch backwards. What if she tried to prove to me that I could do it alone? Like Dad did with the bike?

I hesitated.

I tried to pull out of the skill but I lost my balance. I felt Coach Marie grab my arm but my body had twisted and I fell off the other side of the beam. As I crashed to the ground, my left arm got crushed between my body and the floor.

'Ow!' I yelled, as searing pain shot through my wrist.

'Ella, why did you twist out of the skill? I had you,' Coach Marie said.

'I thought you weren't going to spot me,' I said, as tears pricked my eyes.

'Charlotte, get some ice,' Coach Marie yelled over to Charlotte who was working on the low beam.

I cradled my aching wrist with my other arm.

'Can you move it?' Coach Marie asked me.

I gently tried to move my hand up and down. I could move it, but it was accompanied by a stabbing pain.

'Ouch,' I said, as tears spilled from my eyes.

Charlotte ran back into the gym with an ice pack which Coach Marie then put on my wrist.

'It's swollen. I don't think it's broken, but we can't take the risk,' she said. 'We need to get you up to the school nurse.'

By this point, Mia and Jasmine were sitting by me, gently stroking my other arm.

'You'll be OK, Ella,' Jasmine said soothingly.

'Mia, can you take Ella to the nurse?' Coach Marie asked.

Mia nodded and helped me up. She was careful not to bump my wrist as we stood and she put her arm around my other shoulder in comfort.

We exited the gym together and walked up the path towards the sick bay. Mia held the door open for me as I went inside.

'Oh dear, what have we here?' the nurse said, bustling over to us.

'I fell on my wrist,' I said tearfully.

'Alright, just sit down, Ella, and I'll take a look,' the nurse said kindly.

She gently lifted the ice pack off my arm. My wrist was slightly swollen and was stained red from the cold. She carefully applied a light amount of pressure and manoeuvred my hand, asking if it was painful. I winced and said yes to when it hurt. In this moment, all I wanted was my mum. She'd give me a hug and tell me everything was going to be OK.

'I don't think it is broken—just sprained,' the nurse concluded. 'But we'll need to keep you off it for a little while.'

'But we have a gymnastics competition in two weeks!' I protested.

'It should be OK by then. But in the meantime, you might have to limit the amount of training you do so that you don't overuse it. And I don't want you on it at all for the next few days.'

I nodded mournfully.

'Just stay here and keep the ice pack on it for now. I'll bandage it up shortly,' the nurse said, as she went off into another room.

'Ugh, I can't believe it,' I said.

'At least you can still compete,' Mia said.

'Probably not in the mock comp this weekend though,' I said sadly. I needed all the practice I could get.

Mia sat next to me in silence.

A door from an adjoining room creaked open. It was the office of the school psychologist, Ms Carruthers. She was here to help girls who were having troubles with all kinds of things—homesickness, sadness, working through difficult feelings. I'd seen her once myself when I was having a really tricky time with homesickness back in first term, and she was really good at giving me some activities to do to help me work through it.

'It was good to see you, Grace. You're doing great,' Ms Carruthers said, as she walked out into the main waiting area where Mia and I were sitting.

'Thanks, Ms Carruthers,' Grace said, following her out.

As Grace entered the waiting area, she locked eyes with me and froze. She opened her mouth as if to say something but quickly shut it again. Then she rushed out the door without saying a word.

Why was Grace with Ms Carruthers? And why wouldn't she tell us about it? Lots of my friends had been to see her—it wasn't something to be embarrassed about. Why would Grace keep it a secret? If she was sad or worried or homesick, why wouldn't she tell her friends about it?

Chapter 10

'Is she homesick?' Zoe asked.

I shook my head. 'I asked Grace if she's homesick and she said no. Then I asked her why she was with Ms Carruthers and she said Monty was making her go because of the hat-in-the tree incident.'

'But that was ages ago. And it wasn't even that serious. Why would Monty make Grace see Ms Carruthers about something like that?' Zoe said, puzzled. 'Grace has done a tonne of silly pranks here at Eden, and she's never been sent to Ms Carruthers about it. And anyway, Ms Carruthers doesn't usually do discipline stuff. She's there for—I dunno—more emotional stuff, right?'

Zoe and I continued walking down the path towards the drama studio for our afternoon class. I kept thinking about it as we passed the aquatic centre.

'And why would she be so secretive about it?' I mused. 'We're all pretty good friends now, right? But I outright asked her if something was up and she denied it.'

'I *hate* to butt in,' a voice trilled from behind us.

'Saskia, are you listening in on our private conversation?' I asked, annoyed.

'You talk so loudly, Ella. I'm surprised Grace didn't hear you herself,' Saskia snapped.

I looked around but there was nobody else near us. Zoe and I had thought we were alone, but it was just like Saskia to sneak up and eavesdrop.

'Why would you care anyway?' Zoe said. 'It's not like Grace is one of your best friends. We are just trying to be nice friends.'

'I reckon I know what's wrong with her,' Saskia said.

'But it sounds like you don't want *my* advice,' she said, as she overtook us and started skipping down the path.

I looked at Zoe, trying to read her thoughts.

'Saskia, wait,' I called out.

Saskia stopped in her tracks and turned back around, waiting for us to catch up.

'OK, you win. What do you know?' I demanded.

Saskia looked from me to Zoe. 'You really want to know?'

We nodded.

'I think Grace is leaving Eden College,' she said flatly.

Zoe laughed out loud. 'Leaving? Grace? As if! She would have told us.'

Saskia shook her head. 'I don't think so. She's scared to tell you all because she doesn't want to upset you.'

'And where did you get this information?' I said, disbelievingly.

'I overheard their conversation while I was standing outside Monty's office,' Saskia said, matter-of-factly.

'Why would you be listening in on someone else's conversation?' I said, feeling disappointed that Saskia was spying on my friend.

'Do you want to know the info I have or not?!' Saskia spat back in return.

'So, what did they talk about?' Zoe asked slowly.

'Monty told Grace that Ms Carruthers would support her through the changes in her life as a result of "recent decisions",' Saskia said, using her fingers for air quotes.

I bit my lip. Grace hadn't told us about any changes in her life.

'And Grace even said she was worried about how her friends might react to her "changing things up next year". That's what she actually said,' Saskia said.

'I've already asked Grace what's going on and she never hinted about leaving Eden,' I said, hoping it wasn't true.

'Believe it or not—I don't care. I'm just telling you what I heard,' Saskia said.

'Do you think it's true?' I asked Zoe.

Zoe frowned. She pulled me aside and lowered her voice so that Saskia couldn't hear. 'I don't usually believe much Saskia has to say, but how would she know about

Ms Carruthers? And what did Grace mean about things changing up next year? It does sound pretty convincing.'

'Maybe we need to talk to her again,' I said.

'We've tried,' Zoe protested. 'She doesn't want to tell us,' Zoe said in a louder voice.

'Maybe you need to investigate,' Saskia said, leaning in to our conversation again.

'We're not going to spy on our friend,' I said, narrowing my eyes at Saskia.

'Not *spying*,' Saskia clarified. 'Just . . . watching.'

I glanced at Zoe. She looked unsure.

'I know she is meeting again with Monty in her office this afternoon. We could—I don't know—just happen to be nearby?' Saskia said.

'What do you mean we?' I asked. 'This is *our* friend, not yours.'

'Yes, but I got you the information and, well, I'm a curious cat. I need to know the answer, that's all,' Saskia said, smiling.

'Alright, but only because we want to *help*,' Zoe said. 'It's not like we're doing it to be mean.'

'Meet me outside the dorm house at 4 p.m.,' Saskia said.

As Saskia skipped away I raised my eyebrows at Zoe. Zoe was right—it wasn't like we were spying to be mean. We wanted to help. But something felt really wrong about the way we were doing it. As we walked down to drama class, a knot formed in my stomach. I wasn't sure if this was a good idea. At all.

Chapter 11

'Coo coo!' a voice trilled from the bushes. Saskia was hiding in the garden bed outside Ms Montgomery's window, pretending to be a bird.

'Saskia, we know it's you,' Zoe said flatly as we approached the bush.

'Sssh!' Saskia hissed, dragging us into the bushes with her. 'Monty will hear everything with her window open.'

'This is so dumb,' I said, suddenly regretting our decision to eavesdrop on one of our best friends.

'You want to know if Grace is leaving, right?' Saskia said.

I looked at Zoe, who shrugged.

'Listen!' Saskia whispered as we heard a door close inside Ms Montgomery's office, which was on the bottom floor of the dorm.

I tried to put my ear to the open window but was worried about being seen. It was hard to hear and I could only catch every third word.

'I can't hear anything,' Zoe complained. 'This makes no sense!'

'Just shush, Zoe,' Saskia said.

We leaned in closer to the window.

'. . . but I'll miss . . . friends!' Grace's voice said.

I shot a look at Zoe. Saskia nodded, giving us her best 'I told you so' look.

'. . . best for your educational journey . . . at Eden . . .' Ms Montgomery's voice was low and hard to understand.

Grace was obviously getting upset because her voice became higher pitched and sounded more desperate.

'Ms Carruthers . . . not my fault I'm . . .' her voice cut in and out.

'. . . for your own good,' Ms Montgomery added.

The conversation came to an end and we heard the

door open and close again.

'Case closed. Grace has been expelled and is leaving,' Saskia said, dusting her hands.

'Why do you think she's been expelled?' I said.

'Didn't you hear her? Protesting that it wasn't her fault and she didn't want to leave? And Ms Carruthers is often involved in behavioural management when it comes to expulsions. It all makes sense.'

I looked at Zoe. I hated to admit it, but Saskia's reasoning did make sense. Even if it wasn't expulsion, there was definitely something fishy about Grace leaving Eden. But why wouldn't she tell us?

'Face it, girls,' Saskia said in a mocking tone as she stepped out of the shrub. 'One of your besties is leaving and didn't even tell you. Some friends you all are!'

'We are better friends than you and your friends,' I said, angrily.

'Oh, really? Well, why do you need to spy on your so-called friend to get any information out of them?' Saskia shot back.

Zoe looked horrified.

'Don't be upset, Zoe, she's just being mean,' I said, wondering why Zoe looked so alarmed.

But then I turned around to follow her gaze. Behind me, listening to the whole conversation, was Grace.

'Grace, wait!' Zoe yelled as our friend turned to run from us.

'What are we going to do?' I asked, panicked. Grace knew we were spying on her and she also knew we'd discovered her secret. There was no way she would forgive us. Tears filled my eyes.

'Don't worry, Ella,' Zoe said. 'Let's go and get Violet and Ariel and tell them everything. I think this calls for an EGM.'

That's Emergency Group Meeting.

We ran back to the dorm where Violet and Ariel were playing cards on Violet's bed. We hurriedly filled them in on everything.

'Why would you spy on her?' Violet asked.

'I've tried to confront her and ask her but she just

wouldn't tell me,' I said. 'It was Saskia's idea.'

Ariel looked at me and Zoe with sympathetic eyes. 'Saskia's ideas are never the best,' she said quietly. 'But I understand why you did it.'

'We need to find her,' Zoe said. 'I'm so worried about her.'

'Where would she be?' Ariel asked.

We sat and thought. If Zoe were upset, she'd go to the stables to be with her horse. If I were upset, I would hide in the bell tower with my notebook. Violet often found refuge in the Music rooms, singing and playing piano. And Ariel would probably be bingeing a movie series.

But where would Grace go?

We all looked at each other.

'Art Studios!' we all yelled in unison.

We tore through the school, which was quiet in the late afternoon. Most of the classrooms were locked up, but a few were still left open after school for extracurricular activities. We burst into the Music and Drama Centre and ran up the hallway to the art rooms.

'Girls, no running!' Mrs Hodges said, as we rushed

past her.

We slowed down to a fast-paced walk, but as soon as she turned the corner, we picked back up into a sprint.

We burst into our art room, and sure enough, Grace was inside working on a painting.

I could see from the door that her eyes were red from crying. She flicked paint over the canvas making a beautiful but chaotic piece of art with swirling greys, blues and blacks. It reminded me of a storm over the ocean.

'Grace?' I said quietly.

'Go away,' she sniffed.

We all stood in the doorway.

'We'd really like to come in and talk, if that's OK,' Violet said gently.

Grace looked at Violet then nodded lightly. We all entered the room and sat down at one of the desks.

'Grace, I'm so sorry, we didn't mean to spy,' I blurted out. 'But something has been up with you and no matter how much we asked, you wouldn't tell us. So we . . . we . . .' I trailed off.

'You didn't trust me so you spied. You listened in on my private conversation to get information I wasn't ready to share,' Grace said in a wavering voice.

'We're so ashamed. Please forgive us, Grace,' Zoe said, with tears in her own eyes. 'We were truly worried about you. Saskia told us that you are leaving Eden College, but we didn't believe her until we heard it ourselves.'

'Leaving Eden?' Grace questioned, turning around to face us.

'Leaving, expelled—whatever it is, we are going to miss you so much,' I said.

'I'm not leaving Eden!' Grace said, wiping her eyes. 'Why do you think that?!'

'You said something about how you would miss us, and you've been working with Ms Carruthers. You know I saw you coming out of her office the other day. Have you been expelled, Grace?' I asked, nervously.

Grace stood from her chair and came to sit down at our table. She shook her head and even laughed a little through her tears.

'OK, I can see why you were super worried. I do

forgive you for spying and I'm sorry I've been keeping things from you. But I'm not leaving Eden,' she said.

'You're not?' we chorused.

'No! It's . . . it's something else. But you have to promise not to tell anyone,' she said.

We all nodded solemnly.

'I've been struggling a bit . . . academically,' she said. 'Ms Carruthers has been doing some educational assessments with me.'

'What does that mean?' Ariel asked.

'They want to check in on the way I learn and how my brain works. For some people, our brains just work differently. We learn and take in information differently than others. It can mean we fall behind in school work, but it's not because we're dumb—we just haven't worked out the best way for us to learn,' Grace said.

'You're not dumb!' Zoe said.

'I know I'm not,' Grace answered. 'But, take English for example. Sometimes when I read, the letters get all mixed up on the page. It's hard enough understanding Shakespeare when the words are in the right order!'

‘That must be horrible,’ I said.

Grace nodded. ‘And there’s some other stuff as well about how my brain works when it comes to paying attention. Sometimes I can drift off and not hear instructions. I always just thought I was a daydreamer, but it turns out there might actually be a real reason for why my mind works like that. Ms Carruthers and I are exploring that right now. It’s scary to think I might be different, but also kind of exciting.’

‘Exciting?’ Violet said.

‘Yeah. It means I’m not just lazy or not listening or not understanding. And if we can work out exactly what is going on, Ms Carruthers said we can put special things in place to help me work better,’ Grace said.

‘Why didn’t you tell us? That’s nothing to be ashamed of,’ Zoe said.

‘I know, but I was ashamed. I didn’t want you thinking there was something wrong with me,’ Grace said quietly.

‘Of course there’s nothing *wrong* with you. You’re smart and the most creative person I know,’ I said, putting my hand over Grace's. 'There's nothing wrong with being different.'

'So that's what this was all about?' Ariel said.

Grace nodded.

'But what about when you said you'd miss your friends?' Zoe asked.

Grace's cheeks went pink. 'Oh, that. Um, that's just if they make me change my classes. Which probably won't happen,' she added quickly. She looked down at her hands.

The others nodded in understanding, but I caught a glimpse of hesitation in Grace's eyes.

'Well, you know we are here to support you,' Violet said, standing up to hug Grace.

Zoe and Ariel joined the hug, too. I stood to hug Grace as well, but our eyes locked just as I was leaning in. She looked at me with quiet understanding, like she knew what I was thinking. It was a silent plea, begging me to drop it. I nodded softly and gave her a hug.

Grace knew that I had a feeling she wasn't quite telling us everything.

Chapter 12

From: Ella

Sent: Saturday 7:26 AM

To: Olivia

Subject: Mock Comp Day

Hi Olivia,

Today is *meant* to be the day I do a mock competition with Southern Beaches before the real comp next week. But thanks to my sprained wrist, I can't compete today. BOOORING! Coach Marie said I can come along to practice the dance portion of my floor routine and the parts of my beam routine that don't use my hands, which are the most boring bits anyway. I won't get marked on my routines because it wouldn't be fair, but she said I could film everyone else's routines so we can watch them back to see where we need to improve. So that's me today—camera-lady. I wish my wrist was better. It doesn't even hurt much anymore, but Coach Marie said we can't take any risks before the Interschools comp. I saw a physio in town and they've given me a special strap I have to wear for the next few weeks, including while I'm at the comp.

I hope the other girls in the team do well today. I want to show Alexa and those Southern Beaches girls that Eden College is a genuine threat. It'd be so good to knock them off the top spot.

Better go—the minibus leaves in ten minutes.

Later!

Ella x

'Spray,' I requested, holding my hand outwards.

Jasmine passed me the hairspray and I sprayed it around my head in a hazy cloud, making sure all the stray hairs were slicked back onto my head.

'Can you do my scrunchie?' I asked Charlotte.

She nodded and wound the scrunchie around my bun, making sure it was secure.

I looked at myself in the mirror of the Southern Beaches change room. I wasn't wearing my special glittery long-sleeved leotard today. We were saving that for the Interschools competition. Instead, we wore our training leotards which were a deep, royal metallic blue which shone like glittery marble. Charlotte and Jasmine helped each other with their hair.

'Where's Mia?' I asked.

'I think she was helping her mum in the gym,' Charlotte said.

'I need to go and get the tablet from Coach Marie to film the routines,' I said.

'See you up there,' Jasmine called back as I left.

I walked up the stairs away from the change rooms

and onto the ground floor of the gym. It was quiet, as the gymnasts from both clubs were still getting ready, but I did see a few Southern Beaches coaches walking around.

I rounded the corner and—

'Oof!' I coughed. 'Sorry, Mia, I didn't see you there!'

Mia had rounded the corner so fast that I'd slammed straight into her.

'Sorry, Ella. I was just heading back down to the change rooms to finish getting ready,' she said.

I waved goodbye as she trotted down the stairs behind me.

On the ground floor, I could see through the glass doors into the gym which was eerily quiet. I craned my neck to see into the gym, looking for Coach Marie. I glanced up the next flight of stairs which led to the gallery. Maybe she was up there?

I walked up and the stairs opened out into a large gallery filled with tiered rows of chairs for spectators. I glanced around but the gallery was empty, too. From up here, I could see all the way across the gym.

The Southern Beaches coaches had rearranged it in preparation for our mock competition. Tables and chairs sat in front of each apparatus for the judges.

I turned to go back down the stairs when I saw movement in the gym.

I looked over the railing to see a small figure shuffling around by the vault area. They were wearing a Southern Beaches gymnastics tracksuit, but since they kept their head down, I couldn't see who it was. They looked too small to be a coach.

The figure bent down and pulled a measuring tape along the vaults running strip. Gymnasts often like to measure their run-up to make sure they take the exact amount of steps they need to each time. It's really important for timing your vault. The person seemed to be measuring their run-up, but it was a bit of an odd time to be doing it. They leaned down and rubbed off a chalk marking on the mat. Then they walked a bit further back and marked a new spot on the run-up. That's what gymnasts do to indicate their starting point.

It seemed an odd time to be doing that though. We

would usually mark our run-up during the competition.

'Ella,' a voice called from the staircase behind me.

'Oh, there you are, Coach Marie,' I said. 'I was looking for you so I could get the tablet to film today.'

'Here you go,' she said, extending her arm and passing me the tablet. 'Warm up starts in five minutes, so let's get moving,' she said, smiling.

Just before I went back down the stairs, I took one more look into the gym. The figure suddenly looked up at the gallery and we locked eyes. It was Alexa.

I hit record and held the tablet up so I had a good view of the beam. Mia mounted it gracefully. Her chin was held high and her arms were out with her shoulders pulled back. She looked as elegant as a swan. She began her routine with a leap sequence. Her split leaps were incredible—she did a full split in the air then landed firmly on the beam without a wobble. She moved her arms around in flourishing dance elements. Leaning forward, she completed a handstand, then connected it to a beautiful, high wolf jump. After sticking her jump, she reached tall for a confident back walkover. I winced slightly, thinking about my own walkover and feeling jealous that she could do it with such deftness (which means gracefully and without effort).

Mia moved into a cartwheel towards the end of the beam, then finished her routine with a backward somersault off the end, landing on the mat without a single step. She presented to the judges with a wide smile, knowing she'd smashed the routine.

The judges conferred before holding up her score.

9.45.

The score was out of ten, so this was an excellent score. Anything over 9 was awesome.

'Great job, Mia!' Coach Marie said and Mia smiled back at her mum.

Next was Alexa's turn.

Alexa mounted the beam with confidence. She went through the same movements that Mia had just done. Her style was punchier and less graceful, but she had power and stability. I wasn't filming Alexa's routine, but I watched with eagle eyes to see where the judges might deduct from her score.

At the end of the routine, Alexa did a neat cartwheel then launched off the end, transitioning into a high backward somersault that delivered her to the mat. But Alexa was a bit too powerful and despite remaining on her feet, she took a large step backwards.

The Southern Beaches girls cheered for her as she sat back down with her coach, awaiting her score.

9.2.

I saw Alexa shoot a look at Mia who smiled slyly like a cat. The rivalry between the two girls was on show for everyone to see. The other Southern Beaches girls were doing well, as was Jasmine and Charlotte, but nobody was getting anywhere near the consistent high scores of Mia and Alexa.

So far, Mia was slightly in front on her total score. On floor, Mia been given a 9.2 and Alexa a 9.1. But on bars, Alexa just beat Mia with a 9.6, and Mia a 9.4. It was all going to come down to the last apparatus, which, unfortunately for Mia, was vault.

We walked over to the vault and greeted the judges. I knew I couldn't compete on vault today because of my wrist, so I was there to support the Eden girls and film their vaults.

As I walked over the running strip, I looked down to inspect it. I wasn't sure what I was looking for, but I couldn't stop thinking about Alexa on her own this morning, adjusting the tape and marking a spot. I looked at the measuring tape. It appeared normal.

Jasmine, Mia and Charlotte each marked a spot with a piece of chalk where they would start their run-up. I examined the markings.

'What are you doing?' an airy voice asked behind me.

Alexa.

'Just looking at the measurements,' I said lightly.

'Whatever,' Alexa said flatly.

'Did you change your run-up this morning?' I asked, standing up and facing her.

'Spying on the competition?' she retorted. 'As a matter of fact I did. I've been experimenting with a longer run-up. Not that I owe you an explanation.'

‘Risky to change your run-up right before a comp,’ I replied.

Alexa looked at me and narrowed her eyes. She shot a look at her coach who was standing down the other end of the vault.

‘One warm up vault each,’ the judges called from the table.

I kept eye contact with Alexa, searching face. She turned away from me and lined up for her warm up vault.

The first of the Southern Beaches gymnasts thundered down the vault and hit the board at speed. She sailed over the vault—too high, in my opinion—and landed on the other side where she tumbled forwards onto her hands.

‘Woah—too much there, Winnie,’ the Southern Beaches coach said.

Charlotte warmed up by hitting the board hard. She also seemed really high in the air, so when she popped her hands on the vaulting table, she shot forwards, falling over onto her stomach.

‘Is that board overly bouncy?’ she asked.

Coach Marie shook her head. 'Same board we've been training on for weeks.'

Once everyone had finished warming up, it was time to compete. Each gymnast was given two chances to do their vault and only the higher score would be taken.

Three of the Southern Beaches girls did their vaults, but they all fell on their landings.

It was now Alexa's turn.

Alexa pumped her tiny legs as she approached the vault. She sailed over it and landed perfectly on the other side.

The score came up: 8.8. Jasmine whispered that it was only a little lower than what Alexa usually scored on vault.

Charlotte and Jasmine then did their vaults which they landed, but they both said it felt odd.

Then it was Mia's turn.

Mia flew down the runway and hit the board. It wasn't the best launch, but she managed to flop over to the other side and land on her feet. So while her vault wasn't technically good, she at least made it over the table and landed.

8.1.

Not an awesome score, but it was a big personal improvement for Mia. In her last competition, she only barely made it over the vault and landed on her bottom, scoring a 6.1.

At the end of the morning, Alexa had the highest overall score for the day. And even though Mia had beaten her on a couple of apparatuses, and had scored close on bars, Alexa's vault score was much higher than Mia's and was enough to put her in first place overall.

'Great effort today, girls,' the Southern Beaches coach said to everyone.

'Really proud of all of you,' Coach Marie said. 'I can't wait to see you all bring those skills to the Interschools comp next week. It's going to be a tight one!'

The Eden girls huddled together, congratulating each other on a great competition.

'Your kip on bars was great!' I said to Jasmine. 'All that additional practice really paid off.'

'And Mia—your vault was heaps better!' Charlotte

said, giving her a quick hug. 'I reckon you'll nail that next week, and then you'll best Alexa overall.'

'Did you find anything about vault a bit . . . I dunno . . . odd today?' I asked.

'Yeah, it did feel a little weird. I don't know if it was the board but I was getting way more height than usual—too much height,' Jasmine said.

'Could it have been something to do with the run-up?' I asked.

Charlotte shook her head. 'I don't think so. Or maybe—I don't know. It just felt . . . different.'

'I didn't notice,' Mia said, shrugging.

'Why, Ella?' Jasmine asked.

'I don't know, but this morning I saw Alexa in the gym when nobody was here,' I said, glancing over to the Southern Beaches girls. They were all hugging Alexa and congratulating her on her first place victory. 'She was adjusting the markings on the run-up.'

'So?' Charlotte said. 'That's fine—we are allowed to start wherever we want.'

'Yeah, but isn't it a weird coincidence that she was

doing it before anyone was in? And then everyone's vaults were off? Could she have . . . I dunno . . . *done* something?'

'Like what?' Jasmine said.

I shrugged. I didn't know. But it still felt fishy.

'It's that Eden Press reporter in you,' Mia laughed. 'Always looking for a scandal!'

I smiled at Mia and shook my head. 'You're probably right. I'm sure it's nothing.'

I caught Alexa's eye and she raised an eyebrow at me. Then she turned and walked away.

Chapter 13

'How's the wrist feeling, Ella?' Coach Marie asked.

I used my right hand to squeeze my injured wrist, which was still strapped tightly into the brace the physiotherapist had given me.

'Good,' I said firmly.

I'd been doing special exercises to help strengthen my wrist over the last few days and I'd even started doing more gymnastics on it. I started with easy things like handstands, then I slowly reintroduced bar work and even some light tumbling on floor. Today, I was going to try my vault, as the whole team was working on it together.

We started with some warm up drills, including knees-up running and jumping drills. We also practiced pushing off our hands with straight arms, popping in our shoulders to bounce off the wall.

We then moved over to the vaulting table to work on our vault, which was a fast run-up to jump on the board, then a quick handspring onto the vault with lots of height to pop us over to the other side. In Level 5 we would land on our backs onto a pile of soft crash mats, but for Level 6 we had to land on our feet. This is where Mia was struggling—she wasn't getting enough height off the vault to land properly on the other side.

Charlotte took a strong run-up and sprang firmly off the board. Her hands touched the vault for a brief second before she pushed through her shoulders to pop over onto the other side.

'Nice, Charlotte. Much better than the comp the other day—a lot more controlled,' Coach Marie said approvingly.

Jasmine also performed a solid vault during her

turn—it was much nicer than the one she had done last Saturday.

'These vaults are much better,' Coach Marie said. 'If you perform like this then you'll smash it at Interschools on the weekend.'

My turn.

I took a deep breath, nervous about performing such a skill after my injury.

I shook my arms out by my side then burst into a sprint. I ran as fast as I could towards the board then launched myself onto it in an aggressive jump. As my hands hit the vault I felt a slight twinge in my wrist, but it was pretty minimal. I popped over the top of the vaulting table and landed neatly on the other side.

'How did that feel?' Coach Marie asked.

'Wrist feels pretty good!' I said, happily. At this rate, I'd be competing as normal by the weekend.

'OK, Mia, your turn,' Coach Marie said.

Mia thundered down the run-up and hit the board hard. She reached forward for the vault but stalled in her handstand. It was too slow. She flopped over the other side, landing briefly on her feet before falling onto her bottom.

'Mia! Push through your shoulders! I thought you'd fixed this on the weekend,' Coach Marie said, frustrated.

Mia hit the mat with her fist. 'I'm trying! I just can't get over this table.'

'You can. You just need to remember the basics. Your shape is wrong,' Coach Marie said.

'Just leave me alone!' Mia screamed, running towards the gym door.

'Mia!' Coach Marie yelled after her.

'No!' Mia screamed back, slamming the gym door behind her.

We all stood in silence.

'Do you want me to check if she's OK?' I said in a shaky voice.

Coach Marie looked out of a window and nodded her head. I thought I saw tears in her eyes. 'The rest of you, back to vault.'

I jogged out of the gym, wondering where Mia may have gone. I walked downstairs to the change rooms but

Mia wasn't in there. *Where could she be?*

Outside in the warm afternoon sunshine, I wandered behind the other side of the gym and walked over to the big oak tree. Sure enough, there was Mia, sitting in the boughs of a high branch.

'Mia?' I called.

'How did you know I would be here?' she asked through her sniffles.

I started to climb the tree. 'Gymnasts love climbing—I figured you might have come up here for some space.'

I hung from a branch then did a chin-up to hook my leg over the branch, hauling myself upwards.

'Be careful, Ella. If you fall, my mum will go nuts,' Mia said.

I reached the branch she was sitting on and straddled it while holding onto the branch above.

Mia wiped her tear stained cheeks.

'You know, she just wants to help you. That's kind of what a coach is for,' I said gently.

'But she's not just my coach. She's my *mum*,' Mia said.

'Why does that matter? She's just trying to make you a better gymnast,' I said.

Mia looked at me with one eyebrow arched. 'You don't get it.'

'Get what? What's the problem?' I asked.

Mia sighed. 'When the coach tells you to fix something, it's just to fix a gym skill. But when mum tells me to fix something, it's to fix . . . *me*.'

I frowned, confused.

'You know how I live with just my mum here at Eden College?' Mia said.

I nodded.

'My dad lives on the other side of the state. When he and my mum split up, he moved back to his home town. But did you know I also have a sister?' Mia said.

I looked at her, shocked. In my whole year of knowing Mia, she had never once mentioned a sister. 'You do?'

'Yep, Dani. She's older than me—she's 22 now. But when we were younger, my mum really wanted her to be a gymnast. She was pretty good, too. But she hated gym. Mum said that was OK and she let Dani pick which sport she wanted to do. She chose skiing and became a *really* good skier. Like, state rep level.'

'Cool,' I said.

'Cool for Dad, but not for Mum. Dad is the skier in the family. He and Dani bonded over skiing so much. They spent heaps of time together and then, when my parents split, Dani said she wanted to go with my Dad to live on the other side of the state. Mum was devo,' Mia said, looking down at her hands. 'That's what the empty room in my house is for. It's for Dani.'

'I was only five years old at the time,' Mia continued. 'But I remember the sadness in my mum's face. I even heard her crying on the phone to her sister about how she wished she had bonded with Dani more so that Dani might have chosen her. I decided right there, even though I was only five, that I would become a gymnast. A really good one. And that way, Mum would know that I would never leave her.'

I reached out to touch Mia's hand. 'Mia, that's so lovely. I'm sure it's been a huge comfort for your mum. But remember that she loves you because you are her daughter and not because you're a gymnast.'

'I don't know about that,' Mia said flatly. 'In the lower levels, I'd always win and she'd call me her "little gymnast". I remember seeing the pride on her face. And I knew that our bond over gym could never break.'

I looked down at my hands. It must have been really hard for Mia to think that her mum's happiness depended on her success as a gymnast.

'Why don't you talk to her about it?' I asked.

Mia shook her head. 'I don't want her to think I don't love gym—because I do! And I don't want her thinking that she's pressuring me like those parents who want their kids to be Olympians, regardless of what the kid wants. It's not like that. I just want to do my best and make her proud.'

Mia sniffed and took a deep breath.

'Are you ready to go back in?' I asked.

Mia nodded. 'I need some space for a bit though. Maybe no more vault for now.'

'How about we go through the footage I took from the mock comp last weekend? We can look at your routines and work out where you need to fix things,' I suggested.

'That'd be great. Thanks, Ella. You're a good friend,' Mia smiled.

Coach Marie was fine with my plan, so Mia and I found a spot on the crash mat to lie on our stomachs with the tablet in front of us. I scrolled through the videos for the competition files so that we could look through them.

We started with Mia's floor routine, which was beautiful. She was such a graceful gymnast, full of artistic flair. Her leaps were high and flexible and her tumbling was strong.

'Pause it there,' Mia said.

I paused mid tumbling row.

'Ah, look at how low I am in the back somersault. I would definitely have lost marks there,' she said.

I nodded in agreement. 'Look here,' I said, pointing to her jump with a full turn. She'd landed about three quarters of the way around. 'The judges wouldn't have awarded you the full turn there.'

Mia jumped up and stood on the flat mats next to us. She did the full turn again. 'Better?'

'Heaps better,' I agreed.

She lay back down and watched more of her routine, pausing at different points to critique her own technique.

We did the same for her beam routine before moving on to her bar routine.

'Ah, your cast isn't horizontal. They wouldn't have given you the mark for that,' I said pointing at the screen.

'Totally,' she agreed.

'Your routines are looking so good though,' I said. 'Should we take a look at your vault?'

Mia's eyes widened. 'No, I have had enough of vault for one day.'

'But your vault on the weekend was really good—you stuck it for, like, the first time in ages,' I said, pulling up the video.

'I said I don't want to,' Mia said, a little too aggressively as she hit the tablet's 'off' button.

I looked at her in alarm and her face softened. 'I'm

sorry—I just don't want to see any more vault right now. But I'd love to help you with your back walkover on beam if your wrist is ready for it?'

I nodded gratefully. Even though I was completely petrified to try it again, I knew I had to start sometime. I stood up and Mia and I went over the low beam where she spotted me for the first few. After a short while, I was doing them on the low beam by myself.

By the end of training, we were all exhausted. We warmed down and packed up our things, ready to go back to the dorms. As we left the gym, I glanced back inside and noticed I'd left the tablet sitting on the crash mats. I jogged back inside and grabbed it, slipping it into my bag to give back to Coach Marie the next day.

Once back in my dorm room, I threw my bag on my bed and flopped down onto my back. My muscles were sore from my first proper training session back since my injury. I sat up to unpack my bag and the tablet tumbled out. I turned it on and the video of Mia's vault was still on the screen. I remembered back to what Jasmine said about the vault feeling weird. I pressed play.

Mia's vault wasn't technically great, but she was making it over the table nicely. Charlotte and Jasmine's were all over the place. I replayed each one, zooming in on the run-up and the board to try and see what Alexa—or anyone for that matter—might have done to the apparatus.

I zoomed in again. *What was going on that day?*

'Hi, Ella,' Zoe said, as she walked into the dorm. She was dusty from horse riding, with a big patch of dirt on her jodhpurs. A pang of jealousy shot through me. I wasn't able to ride my horse, Pharaoh, quite as much while I was training for Interschools. I still got out with him for a morning ride in the fresh air, and other girls in the riding team were happy to keep him exercised for me. But it wasn't the same as being able to lazily ride through the trails with him, talking to him and stroking him.

'Tough day at the stables?' I asked, looking at Zoe's dirty riding uniform.

'Fell off Gypsy,' she said flatly, rubbing her thigh.

'Oh my goodness, are you OK?' I asked, jumping off

my bed to go to my friend.

Zoe laughed. 'All good. It was more embarrassing than painful,' she said. 'Gypsy nicked the top of a jump and landed funny. I came off his side and was able to hold on, but then eventually let go. It wasn't a big fall.'

'Scary though,' I said, giving my best friend a quick hug.

'Nothing a shower won't fix,' she said, smiling. 'Wasn't Gypsy's fault anyway. We are trying a higher jump with him and he's still getting used to the height. It's crazy the difference even a few centimetres can make.'

Zoe grabbed her toiletries bag and a towel and headed out to the showers.

Zoe's words echoed in my head. And then it hit me.

I dived back onto my bed and pulled up the footage of the vault again.

'So that's it,' I whispered. 'Alexa. What have you done?'

Chapter 14

'Ella, are you sure?' Jasmine said incredulously.

'Yes, I'm sure. I saw Alexa hovering around the vault alone before our mock competition. And then this happened,' I said, pointing to the tablet.

'It does sound a little like one of your Eden Press scandals,' Charlotte said doubtfully. 'Can I see the footage again?'

I flicked the tablet on and leaned across the seats of the minibus to show Jasmine and Charlotte their vaults from the mock competition.

'Look at the height you are both getting, only to

then fall over on your landings. But you're not falling backwards—you're falling *forwards*,' I said, as I paused the video.

'I have to admit—it does look pretty suss,' Jasmine said quietly. 'Why would we all be making the same mistake of jumping too high?'

'Exactly,' I said. 'It all became clear when I was talking to Zoe. She said her horse, Gypsy, would have trouble with a jump if it moved even a centimetre. Then I thought, why wouldn't gymnasts be the same? What if you weren't jumping too *high*? What if the vault was too *low*?!'

'Why would Alexa lower the vault?' Charlotte said.

'She's tiny!' I exclaimed. 'Vault is the only apparatus where she is at a disadvantage. Vault is hard for all of us—even Mia—but for a tiny gymnast like Alexa? It makes sense that she'd want to lower the vault.'

'But you said she was tampering with the run-up tape before the mock comp. That's got nothing to do with the vault's height,' Jasmine protested.

'I was too far away to see all the details. But she was

hovering around the entire apparatus. She absolutely could have moved it,' I said firmly.

'So, what now?' Charlotte asked. 'Should we tell Coach Marie?'

'We don't have proof,' I said carefully. 'And Coach Marie and Mia are travelling to the Interschools comp by car, so they might not even be there when we arrive. But that also means we have time.'

'Time for what?' Jasmine asked, frowning.

'Time to prove our theory. The gym will have been set up specifically for the Interschools comp today. The coaches would have measured and adjusted all the apparatuses to make sure they are right for today. So if Alexa is going to tamper with it, it will have to be sometime this morning,' I said.

The minibus turned off the main road and onto the winding street that led to the Southern Beaches Gymnastics Club. As the minibus parked, we repacked our stuff into our bags and got ready to disembark. We were supposed to go straight to the change rooms to meet Coach Marie and Mia before getting ready.

So we didn't have much time. I clutched the tablet in my hand—I needed it for proof.

We walked through the building doors and a competition marshal directed us downstairs to the change rooms. Just behind the marshal, I could see through to the gym, which was empty and dim. We nodded to the marshal and walked towards the stairs, but once we rounded the corner we hid behind the wall until he was distracted with the next set of gymnasts entering the building.

When he wasn't looking, we snuck across the hall to the doors of the gym and slipped inside.

The gym was silent. It felt weird to be in a gym with no noise—gyms were usually alive with sounds, with squeals and thumps and cheers and bangs. But right now, it was eerily quiet and dim.

We walked over to the vaulting table to inspect the height.

'Looks to be the right height,' Charlotte said, standing next to it and placing her hand on its surface.

'So, whoever it is, they clearly haven't been here yet,'

Jasmine finished.

'We need to go and get ready soon, which means the perpetrator doesn't have much time left,' I said.

'What happens if no-one comes?' Charlotte asked.

'Then we're wrong and that's that. We'll quickly get ready and have a great comp,' I said.

'And if we're right?' Jasmine asked.

I hadn't really thought about that. What would happen to Alexa once we had proof? Would she be disqualified?

'Let's wait over here,' I said, shaking the thought out of my head. I pointed to some crash mats that were leaning upright against the wall. There was enough space for us to shimmy in behind it and wait without being seen.

We hid in silence. After a short while I started to feel a bit silly. Maybe this was all a big mistake?

'There's someone here,' Charlotte hissed.

The gym door creaked open and someone slipped inside. They were clearly trying not to make a noise. The person was wearing a sports tracksuit top with their hood pulled up. It was too hard to see around the crash mat to work out who it was without being seen. Instead, I pointed the tablet out slightly from behind the mat to start filming. I needed my proof.

'Who is it?' Jasmine hissed.

I waved at her to be quiet. 'I can't tell.'

Charlotte risked peeking around the crash mat. 'I don't think that's Alexa,' she said. 'She's too tall.'

I stuck my head around the edge of the mat, too. I gulped. Charlotte was right, the figure was much taller than Alexa. They crouched down next to the vault table, their face hidden from us, and began to adjust the height setting.

'But if it's not Alexa, then who is it?' Jasmine said.

'You don't think—' I stopped recording. 'Who is the only person that benefited from the lower vault?' I asked, frowning.

'What do you mean?' Charlotte asked.

'Who used to struggle getting over the vault, but then suddenly had no problem making it over at the mock comp?' I said desperately.

'Oh no!' Charlotte breathed. 'What do we do? If it's Mia, and if we expose her, she'll be disqualified!'

A lump formed in my throat. My hands trembled as I held the tablet. Could I turn in my own team member? My friend? But if she was the one doing this, it wasn't right. This was cheating.

Thoughts tumbled around my mind like washing in a machine.

'We need to get out of here,' Charlotte said.

'We need to face Mia,' Jasmine said.

'Then she'll be in trouble!' Charlotte said.

'But she's cheating against us, too! It's not fair!' Jasmine protested.

I looked wildly from one teammate to the other, my mind spinning. I then peeked around the mat again to look at Mia, fiddling with the vaulting table settings. I shook my head. That was when I noticed the mat we were hiding behind was beginning to sag . . .

'Oh no—'

CRASH!

The mat crashed to the floor, exposing the three of

us behind it. Mia quickly stood up, alarmed and locked eyes with me. I stared into Mia's familiar dark green eyes, which were wide with shock.

But it wasn't Mia at all.

Chapter 15

'Coach Marie?' I stammered.

Coach Marie pulled down her hood and looked at the three of us with alarm.

'Girls! What are you doing here? I was just . . . I was just . . . checking the equipment and . . . and all looks good so far,' she stammered.

'Coach,' I said quietly, 'we know what's going on. You're lowering the vault, aren't you?'

Coach Marie sank down to the mat and hid her head in her hands. 'I'm so ashamed,' she whispered.

The gym doors flung open. 'Mum? I've been looking

everywhere for you. What's going on?' It was Mia, standing at the entrance.

She just walked in to see her mum surrounded by her teammates, with her face buried in her hands. It must have looked really weird.

'Did you know about this?' I asked Mia, gesturing to the vault.

'Know about what?' Mia said, confused. Mia genuinely looked like she had no idea what was going on.

'She wasn't involved,' Coach Marie said quickly, looking up at us.

'Mum, what have you done?' Mia asked.

'Mia, I hate seeing you struggle. And you were getting so upset about vault that I just wanted to help you. But I know what I did was wrong. I lowered the vault, Mia. I lowered it for the mock comp so you would get over it. It was stupid and dangerous. I never planned to do it for the Interschools comp. But then you stormed out of training the other day and I just—I just got scared.'

'You were scared?' Mia asked.

Her mum nodded. It's a strange moment when you

realise that your parents are fallible. That's a big word for not-perfect. And there are moments in every kid's life where they are reminded that their parents are humans, too. That they get scared and sad and angry and even make bad decisions.

'I was scared you'd quit gymnastics. And if we didn't have that together, then . . . then maybe you'd move away like Dani . . .' Coach Marie trailed off.

I remembered when Mia told me about her sister who chose to live with their dad instead of their mum. It was obvious that Coach Marie thought that if she and Mia didn't have gym in common, then maybe they'd have nothing in common.

'Mum, I love gym. It's frustrating and challenging but I'm not quitting. And even if I did, that doesn't mean we wouldn't be close anymore. You raised me. It's been you and me for years. I wouldn't want to move away just because of a sport,' Mia said, putting a hand on her mum's shoulder.

In that moment, Coach Marie looked like the child and Mia the adult. It was all backwards and upside-down and topsy-turvy.

Coach Marie pulled her daughter into a hug. But then light suddenly flooded the gym, and the boys' coach, Coach Matt, walked in.

'A little Eden College meeting before the comp?' he asked confused.

I immediately glanced over at Mia, who looked from me to her mum. Charlotte and Jasmine stood in silence. Coach Matt studied all our faces and frowned.

'What's going on?' he asked.

Coach Marie stood up. 'Matt, can we talk? In your office?' she said.

Coach Matt nodded slowly, and then he and Coach Marie walked out of the gym, leaving us behind in a cloud of silence.

I pulled on my long-sleeved competition leotard. It was my first time wearing it in a competition representing Eden College. The royal metallic blue shimmered under the change room lights. The leotard dipped into a deep neckline, lined with shining diamante crystals. Beneath the neckline was an inverted v-shape with white trim, and the bottom half of the leotard was a more vibrant blue with crushed crystals all over it. I ran my fingers over the elegant leotard. It was unlike any leotard I had competed in before.

I looked up at my face in the mirror and gently swept my fringe to the side, securing it with a bobby pin. I had already tamed the rest of my thick brown hair into a tight bun on the top of my head, secured with two elastics, about a thousand bobby pins, a tight velvet blue scrunchie and several cans of hairspray. My fingers touched the rock-solid mass that was my hair, glued down like cement.

'How about a dash of sparkle?' Jasmine said from next to me.

I closed my eyes and she dabbed the tiniest bit of glittered eye shadow on my eyelids.

'Perfect,' she smiled.

The four of us walked upstairs with our arms linked together. We all felt nervous about the competition, but also unsettled and unsure after what happened with Coach Marie. Would she be fired? Would we even have a coach for the competition? Would Mia have to leave Eden College? On top of that, my stomach twisted and turned over the thought of my back walkover on the high beam. While I could easily do the skill—I'd done it a thousand times on the low beam—I still hadn't the confidence to complete one alone on the high beam. A competition seemed like the worst time to test my courage.

'Oh, you girls look beautiful!' a voice gushed.

We turned to see our principal, Mrs Sinclair, standing in the lobby of the gym, beaming from ear to ear.

'I've come to watch you compete, and I couldn't be more proud,' she said. 'Can I have a photo?'

The four of us stood together, arm in arm, smiling at her camera.

'Good luck, girls,' she said. 'I'll be up in the gallery cheering you on.'

'Thanks, Mrs Sinclair,' we chorused as she made her way up the stairs to the gallery.

'She obviously doesn't know about Coach Marie,' Charlotte whispered.

Mia shot us a look.

'Not now,' I whispered back. Charlotte nodded.

We walked inside the gym to the competition area. There were fifteen other teams competing, including Southern Beaches. We moved through our general warm up with no sign of Coach Marie.

Then she came bustling through the gym doors towards us. We ran to her and all four of us hugged her.

'I'm here, girls. I'm here,' she whispered.

'What happened with Coach Matt?' Charlotte asked.

'It's OK, girls. Matt was extremely kind and forgiving. He said my actions could have been dangerous and if he wanted to, he could report me to the gymnastics board.'

Mia took in a sharp breath.

'Matt is disappointed, but he said that it was fortunate my actions hadn't affected the real competition, so he's not going to report me if I promise never to do something like this again. He knows this is very out-of-character for me,' Coach Marie said. She hung her head shamefully.

'The worst part of all of this . . .' her eyes filled with tears. 'Is that I've been a terrible example to my gymnasts and I've let you down. I'm so ashamed and I want each of you to know that cheating is never ever the answer. My actions were based in fear, but I wasn't thinking about how this would affect the rest of you, and that was unfair. I am so sorry, girls.'

We nodded solemnly.

I felt conflicted. By trying to cheat for her daughter, she'd also cheated against us. But my anger ebbed away as I watched Coach Marie pull Mia into a hug. This was never about gym. It was always about her daughter. And her fear of losing her.

'I think we should put this behind us. And go and have the best comp of our lives!' I said.

Coach Marie pulled all four of us into another hug. 'I'm so proud of you all,' she breathed.

The moment was interrupted by a marshal who called for all gymnasts to line up by their first apparatus, which, for Eden College, was the floor. But as we walked over, we saw which club we would be on rotation with—Southern Beaches. Alexa and her team stood in front of the judges, waiting for us to join them. Lining up next to them, I stood on the end of the Eden College team, right next to Alexa.

'Ready to face the Southern Beaches girls today?' she whispered to me.

'You are so ON,' I hissed back.

And that was when I had made a decision. Bravery. As Nanna Kate says, 'don't let fear hold you back.'

I was ready.

Chapter 16

I hate that moment. That one, silent moment. Steadily holding my pose, waiting for the music to signal the start of my routine.

Just breathe.

The music suddenly blared through the system, shocking me into action. I sailed through the dance elements and then stepped into a corner of the mat, giving myself the biggest run-up I could without stepping outside the mat's perimeter.

I let out a breath and ran fast and hard into my first tumbling row. I did two quick handsprings, followed by a cartwheel. Neat. I then listened to the music and leapt through the air like a gazelle—high and graceful. My leaps were beautifully stretched out and I could feel my legs reach a full split in the air. After a few more movements I had reached the other corner of the mat, ready for my next tumbling row. This one was easy. It was just a simple forward somersault, but I had a habit of either over rotating and running out of room for my landing or under-rotating and landing on my bottom.

I raced forward and hit the mats hard with two feet. I reached a nice height then tucked my body into a ball for a single rotation before opening out for a solid landing.

Only two rows left.

I leapt through the air, transitioned from a backward roll into a handstand, then flew through the dance elements of my routine. All I had to do now was nail my last row and it would be a great routine.

Pumping my arms, I ran strong into my final row. I extended my arms out in front of me to launch into a hard and fast round-off (which is like a cartwheel but you land on two feet). Next, a strong backflip, and from its rebound I soared into the air, tucking my body into a backward somersault. But my landing was short and my knees touched the ground.

No!

Touching the ground like that was considered a 'fall' and incurred a big deduction.

The music finished and I presented to the judges.

'Solid routine, Ella!' Mia whispered as I walked back over to my team.

'I can't believe I fell on that last tumbling row. That's so frustrating!' I sulked.

I took a long sip from my drink bottle, focusing anxiously on the score card.

A number appeared.

8.9.

It was actually an excellent score, considering the fall.

'Shake off that fall, Ella,' Coach Marie whispered. 'Don't let it get you down. We need to stay positive.'

I nodded.

Next up was Alexa and she performed a near-flawless routine. Unlike mine, she didn't fall on any of her skills and came out with a 9.4.

'Gymnast number 22,' the judges called.

That was Mia's number.

Mia stood and walked elegantly to the centre of the floor. She presented to the judges, then moved into her opening pose. As Level 6 gymnasts, we all performed the same routine. We weren't a high enough level to choose our own music and routines yet. But it meant it was pretty easy to compare our performances.

Mia was as graceful as a ballerina on her floor routine. She performed the skills in a similar way to Alexa, but Mia had a lot more grace. She was as light as a feather, floating in the breeze. Her somersault looked like she was suspended in the air for an impossible amount of time, and her landing was soft and silent. She finished her routine with a perfect backwards somersault and walked over to our team to take a big sip from her water bottle.

9.6.

'Way to go, Mia!' Jasmine cheered.

Mia beamed.

‘Good job,’ her mum winked.

By the end of the rotation, Mia had the highest score on floor for our group.

We then moved to bars.

My bar routine was solid, gaining me a 9.0 score, but Alexa blitzed all of us with a 9.6. Mia took a big jump on her landing, and while she luckily didn’t fall over, it brought her score down to 9.1 on what was otherwise a beautiful routine. I could see her frustration as she made her final presentation. Alexa chuckled to herself with glee.

Jasmine smashed her personal best score with an 8.8.

‘See? All that work on your kips was worth it!’ Coach Marie smiled.

I looked around the gym at the other school clubs moving through their rotations. Scores were hovering around eight and a half, with some even down in the sixes. It was pretty obvious that the two major contenders for this competition were Eden College and Southern Beaches.

‘OK, off to beam,’ Coach Marie said, as we took our

bar grips off to put them back in the little pouches.

Here we go.

As we walked over to the beams, I kept my focus on the judges. I didn't want to look at Alexa in case she psyched me out. 'Be brave. You can do it,' I kept whispering to myself.

Alexa and Mia were still close, with Mia scoring an 8.9 and Alexa scoring a 9.2. But I didn't want to beat their scores — I just wanted to be able to get through my routine without backing out of my walkover. Oh, and to not fall off and break my wrist, too.

'Ella, look at me,' Mia said, just before I went on. 'You know you can do this. You've done it a thousand times on the low beam. So when you are up there, just keep telling yourself, "I'm on the low beam. I'm by the floor. I'm safe."'

I nodded.

My number was called and I presented to the judges. I mounted the beam gracefully and confidently. Working through my dance movements and leaps, I landed each one nicely. When I did a full turn on one leg, I only wobbled a little at the end of it. My handstand was strong and elegant, finishing tall and proud.

It was time for my back walkover.

I stood tall with my hands in the air.

You are on the low beam. You are brave. You are safe. You can do this.

I closed my eyes, blocking out the crowd and the floor below. I wanted to pretend I was on the low beam. As I arched back, I opened them wide and focused only on my hands as they touched the beam. I grasped it tightly and kicked my legs over.

'Woohoo!' Mia screamed out.

I did it! All by myself!

Bursting into the widest smile, I finished my routine with a cartwheel, followed by a back somersault off the end of the beam. I took a small step on my landing, but even that couldn't crush my spirits.

I presented to the judges with a beaming smile and they even smiled back at me.

My team were on their feet, cheering for me. After running over to them, I glanced up to the gallery where

Mrs Sinclair was standing, applauding.

The score came in: 9.1. I couldn't believe it. It was my highest score of the day so far!

Charlotte, Jasmine, Mia and I made some quick calculations. The Eden and Southern Beaches teams were almost inseparable in their scores. It was all going to come down to our last apparatus.

Vault.

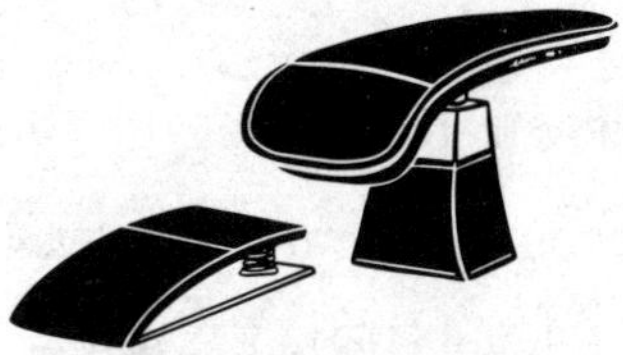

Chapter 17

The first three Southern Beaches girls competed in their vaults, scoring in the high eight to low nine range. It was a solid start. We'd have to give it everything we had to beat them. Especially when Mia was likely to score very low.

Alexa presented to the judges. She ran up the runway, her tiny legs pumping, and hit the board with force. She sailed through the air and landed on the other side, but she took a big step on her landing. My team glanced at each other. It wasn't her best vault and it was unlikely to count, unless something went really wrong on her next attempt.

Alexa stared down the runway, her lips moving silently as she encouraged herself.

She thundered down the mats. But as she approached the board, something about her run-up was off. It seemed like she was on the wrong leg. She did a series of tiny little runs to try and fix her footing, then hit the board softly. She made it over the vault, but didn't get much height. When she landed on her feet she couldn't keep her balance and fell back onto her bottom.

Everyone gasped.

Alexa stood up and presented to the judges. She looked really disappointed.

Fortunately for her, that last vault wouldn't count—the judges only counted the best attempt. Unfortunately, her first vault wasn't her best either.

8.7.

It was a solid score, but a little low for Alexa. She sat down and buried her head in her hands. I could tell she was worried that her chance at winning the individual title had slipped through her fingers.

It was now Mia's turn. 'Mia, do you know what helps me when I do vault?' I whispered to Mia.

She looked at me.

'I channel all my frustrations into a single point on the vault table then I imagine squishing it with my hands as hard as I can. You need to keep your arms straight and push from your shoulders, but you have to smash those feelings out there on the table,' I said. 'I know that sounds silly . . .' I said, trailing off. It was hardly a solid piece of coaching advice. But maybe it was what she needed?

I held my hands up in front of Mia. She pushed against them, her shoulders moving with her.

'Harder,' I said flatly.

She pushed again, this time pressing harder with her hands into mine.

'One more. Push hard. All those times the vault has beaten you. The stress from your mum being your coach. The pressure of beating Alexa. All of it. Smash it,' I said.

She pushed hard against my hands—so hard that I had

to take a step backwards. I nodded at her.

Mia's number was called and she presented to the judges. She stared down the vault with narrowed eyes. She was facing up to her nemesis.

Mia's feet pounded the mat as she sprinted towards the vault. She hit the board hard and flew upside down into a handstand on the vault table then quickly pushed off with all her might. She soared through the air in a beautiful shape, landing neatly on the other side.

She looked at us with wide, surprised eyes. Even Coach Marie looked shocked.

She ran back up the runway for her second attempt, which was a carbon copy of the first. When she stuck her landing, we all ran in and hugged her.

'You did it!' Charlotte yelled.

'I—I guess I did!' Mia said. She bit her lip, staring nervously at the score cards.

The judges whispered to each other. One seemed to have a lot to talk about as they deliberated.

Mia bounced up and down on her toes, anxious to see the score.

The numbers came up.

9.0.

The highest score Mia had ever achieved on vault. She beamed with pride.

Charlotte and Jasmine finished with strong vaults, but Jasmine fell on her landing, costing her a heavy deduction.

Coach Marie walked up to me.

'Ella,' she said slowly. 'I debated whether or not it was helpful for you to know this, but I think it is. You are the kind of gymnast who steps up to a challenge. So . . .'

I looked at her, confused.

'I've been crunching the numbers and I believe you can win us the all-rounder trophy with this vault,' she said.

I looked her in the eyes. I couldn't decide if I was upset at her for putting so much pressure on me, or thankful for knowing exactly what I needed to do. But as Nanna Kate says, knowledge is power. If I knew what I needed, I could aim high.

'What score do I need?' I asked.

‘9.0,’ Coach Marie said. ‘This is well within your capabilities, Ella, which is why I decided to tell you. You just need to do your usual strong vault. Run fast and push through those shoulders. You’ve got this,’ she said, squeezing my arm.

The judges called my number. I stepped up to the starting point and looked at the vault with laser-sharp focus.

I can do this.

I presented to the judges and then focused my attention down the runway. I stared at the board ahead of me. This was my time.

I pumped my arms and legs and then circled my arms around as my two feet hit the board. I pushed off the vault table and maintained a strong shape through the air. The ground quickly came closer and I landed in a deep squat. But my landing wasn’t balanced enough and I took a big step forward.

I swallowed hard.

As I walked back up the runway, Coach Marie ran alongside me.

'Nice vault, Ella. I think that first one would have scored in the high eights. If you can stick this landing, I think you've nailed it,' she whispered.

I nodded silently. I looked up to the gallery where Mrs Sinclair was cheering, then over to my team who were cheering and giving me the thumbs up.

I presented, then proceeded to run-up the mat. Hitting the board hard, I then reached my arms out to hit the vaulting table. I bounced off it with all my strength, soaring into the air . . . I just had to stick this landing.

Just stick it.

I closed my eyes just as the floor met my feet.

Chapter 18

'And the overall standings for Level 6,' the announcer said into the microphone.

'In third place, Merewether College and Gymnastics Club.'

We all applauded as their team stood together on the podium.

'In second place . . .'

I squeezed Jasmine and Mia's hands.

'Southern Beaches College and Gymnastics Club.'

We looked at each other's gleaming eyes.

'In first place, Eden College and Gymnastics Club!'

Squealing, we ran to first place on the podium. We stood next to each other and lifted our joined hands into the air to thank the crowd as it erupted into applause. The head judge shook our hands as he hung a gold medal around each of our necks. I held the cold, heavy medal in the palm of my hand.

Then the head judge presented us with a shiny gold trophy, which would sit on display at Eden College until the following year. We held the trophy high in the air as the crowd, especially Mrs Sinclair, cheered loudly.

The four of us jumped down and hugged again just as Coach Marie came over to join us.

'Thanks to your vault, Ella, we won the overall trophy,' Jasmine said happily. 'You smashed it. 9.3!'

'It wasn't just my vault that did it. We *all* smashed it with our scores,' I replied. But my heart swelled with pride.

'And now for the individual result for Level 6,' the announcer said.

For a competition like Interschools, there were award placings for the schools whose team received the best combined scores as well as awards for the gymnasts with the highest overall scores across the four apparatuses.

'Third place overall, Amelia from Hillcrest Gymnastics!' the announcer said.

The girl stood up and jumped onto the third place podium, waving to her fellow teammates.

'You earned it, Amelia!' they cheered.

'Second place, Mia from Eden College!'

Mia ran up to the podium to receive her silver medal. She beamed from ear to ear. She'd never won an overall place before because her vault had always let her down.

'And first overall, Alexa from Southern Beaches!'

The crowd cheered as Alexa jumped up. She waved to the crowd happily as the head judge hung the gold medal around her neck. She turned to Mia and smiled.

'Good comp,' Mia said, extending her hand.

'Great comp,' Alexa smiled back, shaking Mia's hand.

As Alexa jumped off the podium, there was one more thing I needed to do.

'Uh, Alexa?' I said.

She turned to me. 'Ella, isn't it? Great job today.'

I smiled at her. 'I—I just wanted to say sorry.'

'For what?' she asked, confused.

'I saw you in the gym moving the run-up tape before the mock comp. I told my team that I thought you had tampered with the vault, since everyone was falling all over the place that day. I know I didn't have to tell you this, but I guess my conscience wouldn't let me get away with it. I'm sorry for starting a rumour without proof. I know you didn't do anything to the vault,' I said, sheepishly.

Alexa frowned then broke into a cheeky smile. 'It's OK, Ella. You were right. I was tampering with the run-up,' she said.

'What?!' I exclaimed.

'My coach never lets me have as long a run-up as the other girls. She says I'm too small and not powerful enough in my running. I hate being seen as the baby of the team, just because I'm little. I'm just as old as the rest of them! Anyway, I thought I'd prove her wrong by lengthening my run-up. When it worked out OK, I told my coach but she was annoyed at me for changing it at the last minute. She said messing with the program right before a big comp was a silly idea, and she wanted me to change it back.'

'So, what happened today?' I asked.

'I did the longer run-up again. And it backfired—that last vault was terrible!' she laughed.

I laughed, too.

'I guess it really is better to listen to your coach,' she said.

I waved goodbye to Alexa and walked back over to my team. As I passed Coach Marie, I saw Coach Matt lean in to her and I heard him whisper, 'See? Mia did it all on her own.'

Coach Marie tearfully nodded at her friend as he gave her a little side hug.

Mia walked up to her mum and gave her a big hug.

'Congratulations, sweetie. You deserved it,' Coach Marie said.

'Thanks, Mum,' Mia said. 'I was thinking. Maybe this summer you and I could go on a holiday to the coast. I would really love to learn how to surf, and there are some great waves up north. Would you do that with me?'

Coach Marie smiled a wide smile. 'I'd love to.'

'Five back handsprings into the ocean?' Coach Matt yelled. 'Last one in is a rotten egg!'

We all sprang to life, running down the beach and launching into our roundoffs. I could hear the thump of hands and feet tumbling along the sand as we launched ourselves down the beach.

As I got to my fifth handspring, I hit the water. The tide crashed against my hands and I laughed as I toppled backwards into the water.

'I win!' Alexa yelled.

'As if, Alexa. I smashed you,' Blake from the boys' squad yelled back.

As a celebration, the Eden girls and the Southern Beaches boys' and girls' teams had decided to have a post competition swim at the beach. Coach Matt and Coach Marie had organised it with us beforehand, so we had our swimming costumes with us.

'Watch this!' James said.

He gave Iggy a boost into the air and Iggy did a soaring front somersault, then landed back into the ocean, laughing.

Everyone played in the water, having splashing fights and races up and down the beach. When I was finally exhausted, I flopped down in the sand next to Alexa who was sitting in the wet sand, right at the shoreline. The waves came in and lapped around our bare legs.

'Oh, hi, Ella,' she said. Now that we'd all been playing together at the beach, it seemed like there was no rivalry left between us at all.

'I'm kinda glad that's over,' I said, feeling relief rushing through my body. 'I was so stressed about that back walkover on beam.'

'You were?' Alexa said, looking shocked.

'Absolutely!' I said. 'I've had a mental block on it for ages. The one I did in the comp was the first time I've actually done it alone.'

'You're kidding? We were all really intimated by you Eden girls. We knew you were going to be our toughest competition. And when I saw you climbing the rope, I knew you'd be one of the best,' Alexa said.

'Really?' I said. I couldn't believe it. Alexa had been intimidated by me?! 'I guess it goes to show you never really know what's going on inside someone's head until you actually talk to them!'

Alexa nodded.

I looked out to sea and thought about my friend Grace.

'I guess we'll see you at the next comp,' I said, standing and putting out my hand to help Alexa up.

'One more tumble?' she asked cheekily.

'You're on.'

'What are you going to do with all your spare time now that Interschools is finished?' Ariel asked me as we sat in the afternoon sun back at Eden College.

'I want to get down to the stables to ride Pharaoh more,' I said, wiggling my toes in the sunshine.

'Oh, I just remembered,' Violet interrupted. 'Did you all put down your preferences for a language next year?'

In Year 7, we got to try out three different languages. But for Year 8 we needed to pick one that we liked best to continue with. Even though it wasn't the end of the year yet, we were asked to put our preferences in now so the school could get an idea of the numbers.

'French for me,' I said.

'Italian,' Zoe said.

'Mandarin,' Ariel said.

'I'm doing French, too!' Violet said, looking at me and smiling.

We all turned to Grace.

'Uh . . . um, I'm not quite sure yet,' she mumbled.

'But preferences were due today,' Violet said.

Grace looked around our group of friends then looked down at her hands. 'I guess if there's something I've learned from the most recent . . . events . . . it's that it's better to just be honest with your best friends.'

'What's going on, Grace?' Zoe asked gently.

'You all know I've been working with the educational psychologist to help me work out how my brain learns best,' Grace said.

We all nodded.

'That's not all we've been talking about,' she said slowly.

'Go on,' I said, placing my hand on her leg in support.

'The teachers think that . . . that I might benefit from repeating Year 7,' Grace whispered. Tears filled her eyes. 'That was what I meant when I said I'd miss my friends. You heard right. I might not be with you next year.'

'What? They can't do that!' Ariel screamed.

Grace gestured for her to calm down and lower her voice.

'It's not definite,' she said. 'It's just something we are exploring. It's not what I want, obviously. It's all going to come down to how I go with school this term.'

We sat in a heavy silence.

'Then you know what?' I said, kneeling up on my haunches. 'We are going to help you.'

Zoe's frown turned into a smile. 'Yeah, we'll help you! Between us all, there's no subject we can't ace. I can help you with Maths and Science.'

'And I'm all over English,' I added.

'I can help with Music and History,' Violet said with shining eyes.

'And Drama is my thing,' Ariel added.

Grace looked around the group. 'It's going to be a lot of work.'

'And we are 100% here for you,' I said, leaning in to hug Grace.

Ariel, Zoe and Violet joined the group hug. 'We've got you, Grace,' Zoe whispered.

Grace smiled and closed her eyes. 'I don't know if I can do it. But I *do* know that I have the very best chance with friends like you around.'

Chapter 19

× —

From: Ella

Sent: Friday 3:52 PM

To: Olivia

Subject: Winners are grinners

Hi Olivia,

I still can't believe we won the Interschools Gymnastics Championships. Mrs Sinclair announced it in Assembly, and Charlotte, Mia, Jasmine and I all had to go up the front to be presented with the trophy again. Everyone was cheering and it was mega embarrassing.

The trophy is now in the cabinet in the school office, so anyone visiting the school can see it and my medal is hanging on the noticeboard in my room.

Coach Marie said that we all did so well that we can go up to Level 7 next year! That's going to be massive. And she also said that Coach Matt's boys want a rematch in our strength competition. I reckon with our extra training for Level 7, we'll smash those boys next year!

Oh, and guess what else? You'll never guess so I'll just tell you. After the Interschools competition, the top gymnasts get to compete at the regionals school competition . . . and guess who got in? I'll give you a hint: it rhymes with bee . . . yes, ME! Mia and I both qualified and we'll be on a team with Alexa from Southern Beaches. We talked to her after the comp, and turns out she's not that bad a person after all. I think I was a little too quick to judge her.

I'd better go—I'm meeting Grace in the library to do some English study. I'm going to help her with our Poetry unit.

Love, Ella x

About the Author

Ever since she learnt to hold a pen, Laura Sieveking has loved creating stories. She remembers hiding in her room as a six-year-old, writing a series of books about an unlikely friendship between a princess and a bear.

As an adult, Laura has spent the vast majority of her career working in publishing as an editor. After several years, she decided to put down her red pen and open up her laptop to create books of her own.

Laura's books revolve around all the things she loved as a child—friendships, sport and a little bit of magic. She has written series for early independent readers and middle grade fiction.

She lives in Sydney with her husband and two children, and her fluffy dog who looks like a teddy bear.

ELLA AT EDEN

Read all the Ella at Eden adventures:

New Girl
The Secret Journal
Musical Mystery
Camp Midnight
The School Spy
The London Thief
Eden Stars
The Shadow Pony
Perfect Score
Puppy Rescue
The Missing Piece

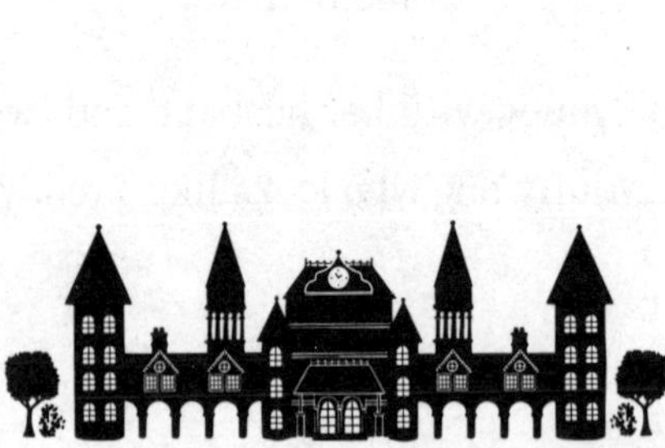